Henniker Secrets

Other novels by Steven P. Marini:

Connections
A Jack Contino Crime Story

   This vigorous, well-plotted crime concoction takes a straight-on look at the tangles and snares involved in stepping outside the "social contract," and it's a kind of morality tale without the classroom lecture. It's pretty well done, too. The author has wisely limited his word count, so it feels just about right, and we're left with the sense of an inaugural job well done.

—The Barnstable Patriot

Aberration
A Jack Contino Crime Story

   Author Marini again shows his mettle when it comes to creating a great storyline . . ."

—The Barnstable Patriot

   Aberration takes off like a bullet with a cool hero: Jack Contino, a cop's cop, who knows a thing or two about criminals, breaking cases and chasing down a cold one. You'll find yourself rooting for him all the way. And if it's the late 1970s you're nostalgic for, you'll feel right at home with this nifty mystery.

—Jordan Rich
Chart Productions, Inc.
WBZ Radio

Calculation
A Jack Contino Crime Story

"Fast paced and suspenseful . . . Skillfully constructed . . . the perfect blending of characters, action and drama gives the reader topnotch entertainment . . . The perfect read for a weekend of enjoyment. . . ."

—Tom Farrell
Massachusetts State Police (Ret)

"A dash of Chandler, a dab of Hammet and a fast paced narrative that will keep you glued to the page. CONNECTIONS is a roller-coaster ride into Boston's past, complete with snappy dialogue, engaging characters and an intriguing plot. If you like crime novels that seamlessly blend violence, sex, and action, this is your kind of novel."

—Arlene Kay
Author of INTRUSION

In Praise of Schmuel's Journey

Schmuel's Journey is an enjoyable thriller set in a small college town in New Hampshire in the seventies. Steven P. Marini immerses the reader in the culture of the time, doing a great job with all the little details. Throw in a couple of murders, fugitive Nazis, and Nazi hunters, and you have all the ingredients for a fun read. Fans of New Hampshire noir will find much to like in this story that keeps the reader guessing right up to the end.

—J.E. Seymour, author of the Kevin Markinson series from Barking Rain Press. *Lead Poisoning* and *Stress Fractures,* available now. *Frostbite*—coming in March of 2016.

In Praise of Henniker Secrets

Steven P. Marini crafts a twist about the eighteenth century New Hampshire legend of Ocean Born Mary. Combining murder, mystery and ghosts, Marini takes us back and forth from 1720 to 1975 for a clever page turner. A highly enjoyable read.
—Barbara Eppich Struna,International best selling author of The Old Cape House and The Old Cape Tea Pot

Henniker Secrets

A Sam and Martha Mystery

by

Steven P. Marini

Gypsy Shadow Publishing

Henniker Secrets

Searching for Truth, Love and Justice Martha Sanborn Travels Through a New Hampshire Ghost Legend A Sam and Martha Mystery by Steven P. Marini

All rights reserved
Copyright © July 20, 2017, Steven P. Marini
Cover Art Copyright © 2017, Elizabeth Moisan
Cover image used with consent from the
Henniker Historical Society

Gypsy Shadow Publishing, LLC.
Lockhart, TX
www.gypsyshadow.com

Names, characters and incidents depicted in this book are products of the author's imagination, or are used fictitiously. Any resemblance to actual events, locales, organizations, or persons, living or dead, is entirely coincidental and beyond the intent of the author or the publisher.

No part of this book may be reproduced or shared by any electronic or mechanical means, including but not limited to printing, file sharing, and email, without prior written permission from Gypsy Shadow Publishing, LLC.

Library of Congress Control Number: 2017951099

eBook ISBN: 978-1-61950-311-3
Print ISBN: 978-1-61950-312-0

Published in the United States of America

First eBook Edition: August 1, 2017
First Print Edition: August 5, 2017

Dedication

To the people of Henniker, New Hampshire,
a beautiful little town

Part One

Chapter One
Early July, 1720, off the New England Coast

"She's no match for us, Captain," said the mate. "We'll be alongside shortly."

The captain kept his gaze on the prey. "Yes, another immigrant ship loaded with fools bound for New England. How good of them to bring us their belongings, everything they own in the world. They'll have no use for any of it where they are going."

"Aye, to the bottom for them," laughed the mate.

The captain nodded, his eyes showing grim determination.

"She's heaving to, sir. We've got her," said the mate.

The calm sea made the task of overtaking the immigrant ship an easy one for the pirate brigantine. Dozens of Scots-Irish people, mostly young families, were headed for a new life in the colonies. They were full of optimism and high spirits, qualities required for those willing to take the gamble of crossing the vast sea in pursuit of a dream. But dreams can be dashed quickly.

"Stand ready with grappling hooks," ordered the young captain, standing tall and confident, as his ship pulled alongside the vessel about to be plundered. His smooth, youthful face had fooled many an enemy in his less than twenty years. But his deep, booming voice and tall, muscular frame served him as a fighter. His intelligence and quick thinking made him a respected leader to those who served under him.

He always hoped to go to sea. He believed, like many an ambitious youth, that nothing would stand in the way of his dream. But he'd never expected to fall in love. A beautiful young lady named Mary, with emerald eyes unlike any he had ever seen, took his heart by storm in his seventeenth year. She changed the course of his life. His love for her was immeasurable. He vowed to spend his years with her, exerting his fullest efforts to earn what would be needed to keep her in comfort and happiness.

For seven months, their love grew. But, as is true with many young lovers, their passion for each other made them blind to the events around them. When sickness took her, his despair was as deep as anyone could imagine. His sadness grew into anger. When a drunken sailor crossed his path one night in a tavern, the young man lost control, his temper erupted and his dagger found the sailor's heart.

In hasty flight, the young man made his way to the docks. He stowed away aboard a tall ship bound for the Caribbean. Though soon discovered, his strength of spirit and strong physique won over the captain, who agreed to allow him to work as a ship's hand and earn his passage. Once in the New World, the young seaman, embittered by the loss of his Mary, took up with pirates. Within a year he rose as a leader, taking his own command. Coveting the coat of a Spaniard who had the name Don Pedro sewn into the left sleeve, he slew the man while attacking the man's ship. From that time forward, his followers called him by that name, Don Pedro.

On Don Pedro's order, the hooks were flung over the side, clutching at the ship full of Ulster immigrants. Their ship was laden with cargo and passengers, not guns. It offered no resistance to the pirates, whose brigantine soon overtook its prey.

Thirty pirates followed Don Pedro onto the captured sloop. They searched for any valued cargo. Three men took over the helm, while the frightened crewmen obeyed orders to drop all sails. Once that was done, movement about the ship was easier, and the pirates went below decks to relieve the schooner of its food stores and fresh water. Passenger belongings were searched. A modest amount of jewelry, silverware and gold coins were found. Pirates took possession of any clothing that suited them, since time at sea wore out such things quickly.

The pirates hauled their catch onto their own ship, using the cases and bags belonging to the passengers as containers. Unwanted items were dropped onto the ship's floor or tossed over the side. "Don Pedro," said one of his mates, "shall we take the flag?" Gazing up at the British banner, Don Pedro laughed. "How many of those do we have in our hold already? No, leave it be. It can rest comfortably on the ocean floor, along with the rest of this mess."

Don Pedro ordered all the sloop's crew amidships. He looked them over, assessing their fitness. "Any of you mates wish to join my crew, you will be welcomed aboard. I can promise you a better life than what you'll get in His Majesty's service. Of course, I'm talking about seamen only. Officers need not apply." The pirate crew burst out in laughter. A handful of the captured crewmen thanked Don Pedro and accepted his offer, pledging their loyalty to him. The rest cursed their shipmates and were restrained from attacking the turncoats by pirate swords held at their bellies.

"Back to our ship, men," cried Don Pedro. "Our work here is done."

"Hold on, there." The captain of the captured ship stepped forward, pushing off the pirates who reached for him. "You've taken all our food and water. You can't expect us to survive out here like that, without rations."

"Oh, good Captain, I don't expect you to survive like that at all," assured Don Pedro, his hands on his hips. "But I'll make it easy and swift for you by sending you to the bottom of the sea."

The remainder of the captured crew quickly reversed their thinking and offered to switch loyalties.

"Ah-ha, too late, gentlemen," cried Don Pedro. "I'm afraid your earlier display of loyalty to your current captain and ship has put you in the *unqualified for duty* category. Off we go."

The captured passengers and seamen fell silent, suddenly taken by the reality before them. In a moment, however, the silence was broken. Don Pedro stopped in his tracks, cocking his head in an effort to hear the noise. He was struck by cries of a baby.

He turned to the doors leading below decks, following the sound to the captain's quarters. Accompanied by a mate, he burst through the doors and stared at the sight before him. A woman lay weeping in the bed, holding a newborn baby. A midwife stood to one side, and the woman's husband to the other. Don Pedro stared at the child as he walked closer to the bed. The midwife shrank away as he moved in. He ordered her to leave the cabin. A pounding started in his chest as he gazed into the eyes of the baby. They were emerald green. His throat went dry and his face turned pale, as if he had seen his Mary reincarnated before him.

No one spoke. Don Pedro eased himself onto the edge of the bed and gently brushed the baby's head of thick red hair with his hand. Withdrawing his hand, he curled it into a fist and pressed his knuckle against his mouth. Memories of his beloved Mary rushed through his brain. His eyes watered. His breathing became labored, and he needed a moment to compose himself before he stood.

"What is your name, good woman?"

"Elizabeth Wilson," she replied. "This is my husband, James," she continued, pointing to him.

"What about the baby, have you named it?"

"No, sir. It's a girl, and we haven't named her yet. We truly hoped for a boy and believed we would have one, so we neglected to choose a girl's name."

Don Pedro motioned for his man. He whispered an order into the crewman's ear. The sailor nodded obedience and rushed away.

The pirate captain stood tall, his body stiff. His jaw tightened. In a moment, after again gazing into the child's eyes, he spoke. "Listen to me and listen carefully." He looked at Elizabeth Wilson and motioned her husband to sit at her side. "I will spare this ship and all the people on board under the following conditions. First, you must give me your solemn word that you will name this child Mary. Do not ask me why. I have my reasons, and they are mine alone." His eyes went to his mates, who stood in the doorway. "I will tell you my second condition momentarily, when my crewmate returns."

James and Elizabeth Wilson stared into each other's eyes, clutching their hands. All were silent until Don Pedro's mate returned. A leather bag was at his side. He offered it to his captain, who received it gently into his hands. The pirate unhitched the strap that sealed the bag and eased his hand inside, withdrawing from it a bundle of green Chinese silk.

"My other condition is that you promise that on the day of her wedding, she will wear a gown made of this cloth, the color of her eyes. Promise me these things, and you all will be allowed to live. I will return half of your food and water. Do you agree?"

The coupled nodded. Tears filled their eyes, and Elizabeth clutched her baby to her breast.

Don Pedro took one last look into the child's eyes, entranced by the emerald green hue. He then turned and sped away. In a few moments, the pirate and his ship were gone, leaving the stunned captives relieved after their close call with death.

Chapter Two
Henniker, New Hampshire, July 7, 1975

Here I was, thirty-something Martha Sanborn, waiting for Sam on a Friday night in July. I was grateful it was the weekend.

He arrived at my two-story apartment at six o'clock, wearing jean shorts, sandals and a yellow golf shirt. He had showered and shaven, and was relaxed and ready for his night with me. I felt like a young woman about to enjoy a weekend thrill with my guy. He rang the bell before entering.

I was barefoot, wearing tight cutoffs and working a hand towel as I appeared from the kitchen. "How many times do I have to tell you there's no need to ring, silly?"

Sam shook his head as he strolled toward me, sweeping me up in an embrace. I flung my arms around his neck. He pulled me up, and my feet left the floor.

"Old habit, I guess," he said. Our kiss was long and lustful. As he let me slide back onto my feet, his hands caressed my backside. He sniffed the air. "What's cookin', my lady?"

"That's a roast. I've had it in the slow-cooker since around noon. Real easy. It cooks while we're at work and is just about ready when I get home. And the place smells great as a bonus." I hugged and kissed him again before easing away. "Let's not let the dinner overcook."

"Luckily for your cooking plans, I'm hungry as a horse," he said. "Let's take one treat at a time."

"Okay, big guy, why don't you go put the roast on a platter, and I'll open some wine. We can eat at the kitchen table tonight. The places are all set. Just carve up some beef and spoon out the veggies. How about a pinot noir?"

"That works," said Sam as he followed my instructions. In just a moment we were seated and enjoying our meal and the start of a summer weekend. Then the phone rang.

I shrugged, as if I had no idea who might be calling. I pushed away from the table and made it to the wall phone across the room in three rings.

"Hello, Martha Sanborn."

"Hey, Mart, it's brother Bart. How's it going?" Bart used his pet name for me. He was the only family member who ever called me that, playing off his own name.

"Well, what do you know? You're alive," I said.

"Okay, okay, don't rub it in. I know I'm not good at keeping in touch."

I looked over at Sam to show my surprised face. He acknowledged me and went back to carving the roast.

"To what do I owe this untimely call, big brother?"

"Untimely? Uh oh, I hope you aren't in the middle of maneuvers, if you get my drift."

"No, Bart. Sam and I just sat down to dinner. But that's all right. It's always good to hear from family. It doesn't happen that often."

"Well, I'll be brief. Don't want your dinner to get cold. I just wanted to see if you'll be around tomorrow. I've got some news for you and thought I'd stop by for a visit. Early afternoon be okay?"

I gazed at Sam again while speaking. "Yeah, early afternoon will be fine. I'll be here. It'll be good to see you, Bart. Where are you now? What's the big surprise?"

"I'm in Boston with friends. Hey, I can't tell you the news over the phone or it won't be a surprise. It'll be a quick visit. I got a lot going on right now, so don't fix any food or anything like that. I can't wait to see you, Mart."

"Likewise, big brother. Okay, no more questions. I'll hold 'em all for tomorrow. Can you give me an idea of what is early afternoon?"

"Oh, I'd say between one-thirty and two," said Bart.

"Fine," said Martha. "See you then."

I eased the phone back onto its holder and rejoined Sam at the small table. "Well, at least I pinned him down to a reasonable time. He usually shows up anytime he chooses."

Sam had met my brother once the previous year. The murder in Henniker, and everything surrounding it, caught his attention, and he showed up unexpectedly to check on his little sister. Sam wasn't overly impressed with Bart, but could clearly see I loved my brother—even if my respect for his wandering lifestyle and lousy business track record was not high.

I saw Sam's less-than-excited expression. "Don't worry, mister. You don't have to be here for the family reunion."

"That's all right, dear Martha. I know you care a lot for him, and I'll be glad to say hello. It should be a fun time for you, and I'd like to participate. It'll be good. What's the special occasion?"

I sighed and helped myself to the food. I took my time filling a plate with about half as much dinner as Sam's portion. "He didn't want to tell me over the phone. He said it was a surprise and didn't want to spoil it."

Sam sipped his wine between swallowing some roast. "You think he's finally getting married, perhaps?"

The idea snuck up on me. "Gee, I didn't think of that. That would be great news. He could use a good woman at his side, like a lot of guys." My eyes glared at Sam like a laser beam.

"What are you looking at me for? I've got one by my side, and I know it."

I grinned and raised my wine glass. "Here's to good partnerships, Sammy."

Our glasses touched with a soft tinkle.

"But seriously, it really would be a good move for Bart. He's had so many screw ups in his life, including bad choices with women and business deals that went sour. Even the ones that start out okay eventually go south. I just don't know where he goes wrong. He's bright and personable, but just can't seem to pull things together in the long run. I hope that whatever this is about, it's positive."

Sam gave me a short smile as he worked down more dinner.

After our dinner was done and the dishes cleaned, we refreshed our wine glasses and moved to the living room, where I turned on the television. Watching the local news for a while gave us a chance to let our dinner settle. Soon we were closer together and decided that there was a better way to entertain ourselves.

Saturday morning arrived with bright sunshine and warm air, not overly hot, just comfortably warm. The humidity was low. Everything pointed to a good day ahead.

By noontime, I had cleaned the downstairs and went out with Sam for some snacks and a six-pack of beer, just in case brother Bart wanted some. He liked Molson's.

The downtown area was quiet, what with it being a July weekend in a college town. Sam found an open parking space right in front of Papa's Market and Deli, which occupied the same building as the pharmacy in an old, two-story wooden building in the center of town. As we left his car and made our way to the storefront door, Sam spied a large figure coming through it.

Ian Barnstead was Sam's best friend in Henniker. He was the head of the History Department. Tall and husky, Ian had a booming voice and a self-deprecating sense of humor.

"How goes it, Mr. Sam, Martha? Staying out of trouble, are you?"

"So far, so good, but the day is young," said Sam.

"Oh, oh. That sounds like something's brewing."

"Just an expression, old buddy. I'm cool."

Sam's expression didn't convince Ian.

"Somehow, Sam, I think you've got something going. You sure you don't have some new adventure up your sleeve? One minute you're the coolest guy on the planet, and the next you're knee deep in something top secret. I don't know." Ian shook his head.

"Oh, it's nothing," I said. "I'm getting a visit from my brother, Bart, today. That's all. I got a surprise call from him last night. I'm getting some beer and stuff so I can be a good hostess."

Ian put his hands on his hips and stretched his body, as if trying the reach his full height. The grin left his face. Ian was familiar with my brother and his reputation. I know he saw Bart as a ne'er-do-well.

"Oh boy, I hope this isn't the start of another one of his schemes. Keep your money in your pocket, both of you." He looked right at me. "You're a smart lady, Martha, but sisterly love can blind a person. I don't know. See you later."

I forced a smile as Ian moved on. We went into the market and fetched the six-pack, along with chips and dip. A moment later we were winding through the Henniker roads in Sam's car, back to my place.

"I know Ian is better acquainted with your brother than I am and we both know Ian is a good guy. I think he was just showing concern."

"I know, Sam. I know."

Chapter Three
Saturday Afternoon, Henniker, New Hampshire, July 12, 1975

I was washing my hands in the kitchen when I heard Sam answer the door. The sound of Bart's voice warmed me. I couldn't believe I was going to see him again. *Twice in one year. Wow! That doesn't happen often.* I rushed to meet him at the door and was swept up in a bear hug from my big brother. *What a bright and wonderful day.*

Then a dark shadow appeared, dimming the brightness. Emerging through the door behind Bart was Auggie Raymond, Bart's childhood friend. I use the term loosely, because the level of Auggie's friendship often fell suspect. He usually got Bart to go along with any scheme he came up with, but sometimes he made Bart so angry I thought he wanted to kill Auggie. Why Bart kept up the friendship, I'll never know.

"Martha, you remember Auggie," said Bart.

"Yes, of course," I said, avoiding his attempt at a hug. Instead, I extended my arm, offering a weak handshake.

"And this is her friend, Sam Miller," said Bart.

"I've heard a lot about you, Sam. That business last year with the escaped Nazi was big news for this little town. Heck, it was big news anywhere. I'm sure glad everything worked out well for you." Auggie shook Sam's hand, gripping it with both of his. He was small, not much taller than me, and about five or six inches shorter than Sam and Bart.

After an awkward silence, Sam motioned to the living room. "Why don't we go sit, and you can tell Martha your big surprise," said Sam. We took up places on the sofa, with Sam at one end and me in the middle. Brother Bart and Auggie took the two chairs across the room; a recliner for Bart, and a rocker for Auggie.

"Sam thought maybe you were going to tell us you'd met the girl of your dreams and were getting married." I turned to Auggie and back to Bart. "But I guess not. So, what's up, Mister Bart?"

Her brother inched forward in his chair, as if getting ready to drop a bombshell. He did, sort of.

"Mart, you know the old Wallace house, the one called The Ocean Born Mary House? Well, we bought it." Bart sounded as excited as a little kid who had just won a contest.

All the blood drained out of my face, and I sat there dumbfounded.

"Shit, Martha, you look like I just said I killed somebody. This is good news, don't you see?"

I shot a gaze at Sam, who looked back at me with a puzzled face.

"No, I don't see, Bart. That old firetrap has been vacant for years, and it's just as well."

Finally, Sam chimed in. "Isn't Ocean Born Mary the baby who was born at sea and is now a ghost haunting her old house, according to legend?"

"You've got to be kidding, Bart," I said. "Why would you buy that place? What are you going to do with it? Where'd you get the money?"

"One question at a time, sister. Auggie and I are going into this as a business venture, a sixty-forty split, since I put up the money. Auggie will split his share with his mother. We've set it up as a corporation. We're sure we can hit it big."

Sam sat forward, clasping his hands at his waist. "I think I know what Bart is going to do, Martha. There must be a lot of acreage with that place. It was an old farm, I understand. You guys must be planning on subdividing the land and developing it with new housing. Am I right?"

I felt a tingle of optimism, but it vanished in a heartbeat when Bart shook his head.

"No, no, that's not it. Besides, that sounds like a lot of work. What we have in mind will be like taking candy from a baby. Look, it's the Ocean Born Mary House, for crying out loud. It's famous, a legend. There are books written about it. People still come by to see it, even though it's not open to the public. Well, we're going to reopen it."

"Oh my God," I said, dropping my head into my hands. "This time I think you've really lost it." My day started with sunshine, but it turned to rain in a hurry. "Bart, that legend idea was started forty years ago by that old coot, Allan Royston, who used to own the house and lived there with his mother. Yes, there was a Mary Wallace who was born at sea under strange circumstances, and she lived in Henniker late in her life, but Royston made up all that nonsense about ghosts and pirates and treasure, for Christ sake. Check it out at the Henniker Historical Society."

I barely got the words out before Bart replied. "We already did. We know all about Royston and his stories. But that was a long time ago. Fact is, we think he did us a favor. He laid the ground work for us. Today, we have network television that can cover stories from all over the world. And we're just over an hour's drive from Boston, a top-ten media market in this country. I know a guy in Boston who is real big with people who follow the occult. He's agreed to help us with our promotion. Do you know that there are college courses on the occult? Heck, there are students and teachers who suck this stuff up and will love coming up here to check the place out. I'm going to write stories and press releases to publicize the legend of Ocean Born Mary. We'll make souvenirs and trinkets of all kinds, pamphlets with pictures for the tourists. Oh, did I mention that we'll conduct tours of the house and grounds? We'll sell that idea aggressively, booking groups from all over, but especially the Boston academic population. It'll be great."

My mouth went dry. I struggled to work up some saliva to moisten my mouth before I could speak. "Where did you get the money for this?"

"Hell, little sister, I know you think I'm a failure, but I've made some cash over the years. I made the down payment, and Auggie and I have enough cash flow to handle the updates and payments until the business takes off. We've got it covered."

I couldn't believe what I was hearing. Bart believed that he and his poor excuse for a partner could make a go of an old, dried up legend. Part of me wanted to believe that Bart was on to something, but it didn't seem possible that his idea would work. "Are you going to live in the house?"

"Yep, for a while anyway," said Bart. "Me, Auggie and his mom. We're fixing up the place now, and we'll be moved in soon."

I glared at Auggie. He had been quiet until now. His mom was as shady as her son, and her name used to pop up now and then in the Manchester newspaper. "That's right," said Auggie. "Mom's agreed to live there and help out with the tours. We'll dress her up in colonial type clothing to add to the atmosphere of the place. Mom's a sharp cookie, despite getting along in years, and she'll be a real asset. She studied up on the legend at the Historical Society and is anxious to help out."

I decided to press about the financial part of the deal. Bart seemed to be taking all the risk in this venture. "So you've had some successes, huh, Bart? What kind?"

I guess I hit a sensitive spot, and Bart decided to move on. He gave Auggie a nod and they stood up simultaneously. "Like I said, dear sister, I've done okay lately. But I'm not going to bore you with that. We've got a guy working on the place right now, and we need to check in on him. You know, see how everything's going. Then we're heading back to Boston. But like I said, we'll be moving in real soon, probably a week or two. Hey, nice to see you again, Mart. You, too, Sam. I'll be in touch."

After a hug from my brother and handshakes for Sam, Auggie and Bart were out the door in a flash. I couldn't hide my disappointment or my concern. This had trouble written all over it.

Chapter Four
Londonderry, New Hampshire, June, 1741

Mary Wilson, a tall and strikingly beautiful young woman, strolled along the walkway around the perimeter of Londonderry Common with her mother, Elizabeth. The late spring weather was warm, and the sun was bright. The townsfolk were delighted. It seemed to please the cattle grazing on the Common as well, since the rains had nourished the grass on which they fed. A breeze caught Mary's long, red hair. She had to draw it back out of her face.

The women were headed for The Gregg House. It was a centerpiece in Londonderry, serving as a stagecoach stop and mail exchange. Besides a livery, it housed a tavern. That was a popular place for gentlemen to meet. They engaged in discussions of interest, usually business, the state of the colonies and whatever achievements a man wanted to brag about. Sometimes women visited the tavern, but never alone.

"How many of your family are still in Ulster, Mother? I know you correspond often with your cousin Karen, and you've mentioned her brother Thomas, but are there any others?" Mary was the only child of Elizabeth and James Wilson. As such, she received devoted attention from her mother, especially since James had died when Mary was only two years of age. Elizabeth took Mary from Boston and moved to Londonderry, New Hampshire, to claim the land granted to her husband, the reason they had left Ireland. Opportunity knocked in the colonies, and the young widow was determined not to lose it despite her husband's passing. Mary grew up yearning for a household with other children in her life and developed a natural curiosity about her relatives in the old country.

"It's getting hard to keep track, because Karen has seven children of her own now, or is it eight? I don't know how they manage."

"Why don't they want to come here like we did? They could live close to us, and I could help her look after all those little cousins. I wouldn't mind doing that, Mother, I truly wouldn't. It would be fun."

"That's generous thinking, Mary, and you would enjoy the family, but you will marry one day soon, I'm sure, and you'll soon have a family of your own." Elizabeth yearned for the day her Mary would be wed. "Cousin Karen leads a hard but happy life in Ulster, and I'm afraid that moving to the New World is not a likely prospect for her. What's more, you are learning about our orchard and the business of running it. You're busy enough with that."

Mary smiled as they continued their walk. They entered the Gregg House and waited behind three other people who were receiving their mail. One was James Wallace, a man eight years older than Mary, tall and broad shouldered. Mary eyed him, like she had done as a young girl admiring an older boy. He had never married.

"Welcome home, James," said the clerk standing behind the counter that separated the mail receiving and storage area from the small lobby. "You seem to be out of Londonderry more than you are in it. I trust the business is going well?"

"Yes indeed," said James, smiling. "We've added plum and pear trees to our orchards, and we expect a hardy crop once they mature. I hope to expand our land holdings someday."

The clerk smiled as he handed Wallace his mail. "Perhaps Mrs. Wilson, there behind you, will consider selling to you one day. You never know."

Mary saw her mother was startled to hear her name mentioned in the conversation. *Sell the farm?* she thought. *Mother would never do that.*

James turned back, trying to spot the woman. He nodded to Elizabeth, to whom he was not well acquainted. When his eyes fell on the tall young woman beside her, his eyes widened and his jaw dropped. "Ga, good day," he said. Speaking became a struggle.

Wallace took his mail and stepped out of the way, allowing the two people behind him to approach the clerk. Mary and her mother stepped up in the line, and James took a position beside them, with Mary next to him. He spoke a greeting to Elizabeth, but his eyes never left Mary.

"How nice to see you, Mrs. Wilson. I trust you are well."

"Yes, we are fine, thank you, Mr. Wallace. I'm sure you remember my daughter, Mary."

"Mary?" He held his hand out, palm down, indicating height. "The last time I saw you, you were about *this* high. My, you've grown so fast and have become a young woman. And a lovely one at that." He said it as a matter of fact, not in flirtation.

"I'll take that as a compliment, Mr. Wallace. Thank you," she said.

Mary saw Wallace search for a way to extend this time in her company. "Are you seriously considering selling your property, Mrs. Wilson?"

"No, not really. I believe the clerk was just being mischievous, Mr. Wallace."

"Please, let's not be so formal. Call me James." He said, still staring at Mary. "Your green eyes are most pleasant."

She noticed him give a quick glance at her ring finger, making her single status evident.

"Ladies, this is a fine summer day, and the evening should be most pleasant. Perhaps you would join me for dinner at my house tonight. I'll send my man, Toney, to fetch you both."

Mary looked at her mother. She showed pleasure at the invitation. Elizabeth felt that something very good might come of this invitation, so she accepted.

"Fine then," said James. "He'll be at your house at seven. I know where it is, and I'll instruct Toney. See you tonight."

Mary was amused when he began tapping the mail envelopes against his hand and a broad smile crossed his face. James bent slightly at the waist before making his exit.

That first dinner became one of many for Mary Wilson and James Wallace. The couple were seen together regularly on Londonderry Common. The two spent as much time together as possible. They were in love, and before the fall harvest James Wallace asked Mary to be his bride.

The winter was cold and long, but it gave Elizabeth the time she needed to make the dress for Mary's wedding. She toiled at it in the evenings, after tending to the business of running her small orchards and farm. She was a skilled seamstress and took pleasure in the work.

In June of 1742, the population of Londonderry lived in anticipation of the marriage of the two successful families. James was the eldest of three sons and had begun running the Wallace farm after the death of his father ten years earlier. The Londonderry Times newspaper ran the announcement of the wedding a month in advance.

On the day of the ceremony, the nervous groom stood at the church altar, awaiting the appearance of his bride. When the organist began to play, all heads turned toward the aisle. Sunlight beamed through a window and shown upon her as she made her entrance. The guests seemed to exhale simultaneously in a gasp at the great sight before them. The bride stood tall and beautiful, her red hair brightened by the sun, and her dress of emerald green silk was as lovely a dress as any had ever seen. She was stunning.

Elizabeth's promise to the pirate, Don Pedro, had been fulfilled.

Chapter Five
Saturday Afternoon, Henniker, New Hampshire, July 12, 1975

"Maybe we should go along with them to see the place. I've never seen a legend before," said Sam.

I ruled that out immediately. "No, Sam, they were trying to cut off discussion and get away. Maybe we'll take a ride by later. I know where it is, although I haven't been there in a long time. No reason to until now. Let Bart and Auggie go do whatever they're up to next."

"Well, then, how about you tell me more about this Ocean Born Mary stuff? I've heard a little about it, but I never paid attention when people talked about it. I plead ignorance, so what can you tell me?"

We parked ourselves at the kitchen table. I poured coffee for both of us as I proceeded to fill Sam in on the legend. Sam liked to get into the details of an issue once he got interested. This was a good sign. Interest led to involvement, and I wanted Sam to be involved.

"So, there really was such a woman? And she's buried right here in Henniker?"

"Yep. You've walked right past her grave many times. It's right there in that old graveyard past the college library, near the baseball field. The legend has many variations, thanks mostly to that old coot, Allan Royston, and his attempts at hoodwinking people. I'm sure you can find out all you'd want to know at the Historical Society. They have some artifacts and drawings over there. Go take a look sometime."

"Perhaps I will," said Sam.

My face showed my disappointment in the turn my brother's visit had taken. This didn't escape Sam. He was getting good at reading me.

"This didn't turn out to be the fun day you were hoping for, Martha, and I'm sorry about that. I think your brother actually thought he was bringing you good news."

I reached across the table and took Sam's hand. His tenderness was always there when I needed it. "Thanks, Sam. You're a great pal."

I kept the language on a level we had both come to accept. If I told him how I really felt, I feared he'd crawl into a shell that I'd never crack. I know who occupied his deepest thoughts.

Carol Vasile was a beautiful woman who had been married to a monster, an escaped Nazi doctor guilty of atrocities against the Jews at Auschwitz, where Sam and his mom were imprisoned in 1944. After surviving that experience and losing his mother, Sam tried to put it all behind him. But events have a way of catching up with you sometimes, and they had caught up to him here in Henniker.

It was hard for Sam to teach Carol the reality of her situation. He had fallen in love with her, but realized she was devoted to her husband, Arthur. When it was all over, she hated Sam, hated Arthur, hated Henniker and left town without looking back, even though Sam had saved her life.

I had known many men, even made the mistake of marrying once. What a sleazebag he turned out to be. Collecting girlfriends was his hobby. But I think he hurt them more than he hurt me. When we divorced, he was glad to disappear. He was never so uncomfortable as when he was with his wife. He didn't have much money, so there was nothing for me to take. I just wanted him gone.

Sam had been divorced, too. From what he told me, she was a climber, and he didn't climb high enough for her. She bed-hopped until she found the type she wanted.

I stared at Sam, and soon our eyes caught each other's. "Tell me, Sam, which ones are we, the young or the restless?" There was a silence before we broke out laughing. His face flushed, and he looked down with an *aw-shucks* grin like he was Gary Cooper. Here he was, trying to cheer me up, when he was the one with a broken heart.

"I know you think of her a lot, Sam. I can almost read it on your face. That's okay, because we're good medicine for each other. We're here to fix things up when they need fixing. I guess I expected too much from Bart, and I set myself up for a fall. And here you are, so sensitive to my situation." I stopped right there before I got sappy.

"Your brother's not a bad guy. Maybe he does some stupid things, but hey, this might work out for him. He's showing some entrepreneurial spirit. You know, if this tourist trap thing fails, maybe he'll think about doing what I suggested."

I nodded my head in half agreement. "You mean subdividing the land and selling it off, maybe developing some houses there? I don't know, but at least it gives him a fallback option, unless—" I wasn't going to finish the sentence, but Sam's eyes cut into me like daggers. He wanted to know more.

"Unless what, Martha? Where are you headed?"

"I was just thinking, well his buddy Auggie isn't a great influence. He's always taken advantage of Bart and manipulated him. It really bothers me that he put up the down payment for this, and yet Auggie is part owner."

"I guess Bart trusts Auggie enough to do that," said Sam. "I gather they've known each other a long time."

"Yes, since the sixth grade. But what I remember is Auggie was always using Bart. That's my opinion, anyway. If Bart got into trouble about something—anything—Auggie was at the heart of it. But Auggie always seemed to come up smelling like a rose, while Bart was the fertilizer."

"What kind of trouble, Martha? Did it involve the police?"

"No, not at a young age. I'm talking about small stuff, you know, like the time Auggie broke a window in our house. They were playing Wiffle Ball in our yard, and Auggie lost control of his bat and sent it flying through a window. He convinced Bart to take the fall with Dad. They were teenagers at the time and having a car was a big deal. Auggie had a car and Bart didn't. He didn't even have his license yet. So Auggie persuaded Bart that he should say he did it. His reasoning was that my parents didn't like him and Bart would be barred from hanging out with him, meaning no riding around together getting booze and girls. He convinced Bart that the blame would wear off quickly anyway. So, Bart took the heat but was still able to get into mischief with Auggie."

"Sounds like Auggie is quite the manipulator," said Sam. "People like that can be dangerous. They put up a false front."

"Eventually it got worse. Auggie ran a scam using chain letters, which are illegal. He sent these letters around to people Bart knew. They tell people to send a check for five dollars made out to cash to the five names on the letter, and the person is supposed to add his own name to the bottom of the list. Each person who receives a letter is supposed to repeat the process, moving the names up the list and adding their own. Auggie wrote up these letters, and his name was always at the top of the list. He never sent any money out, but was always the first to get some back. He lied to people about having received the chain letter, when he, in fact, started the whole thing. The chain would only run a short course anyway, because it would be broken quickly, running out of steam. He'd make a few bucks and then destroy his letters before the post office found out about it from people complaining. He's a beauty, that Auggie."

"So why did Bart stay friends with this guy? Sounds like he was always getting the short stick from his so-called friend."

"I don't know. Bart's a bright guy and always did well in school, but he stuck by his friend. I guess Bart always thought Auggie was cool because of the schemes he would think up. Nothing's changed."

"Let's hope that you're wrong. They got mortgage approval, so it must be a good risk as far as the bank is concerned."

"Maybe, but I'm sure the bank will be happy to foreclose on default and resell the 130 acres. I don't like any of it."

Sam slid out of his chair, pushing away from the table. He took my hands and eased me onto my feet in front of him. I felt warm as he wrapped his arms around me. He pressed me close. I closed my eyes with my head nuzzled into his chest, arms around his neck, enjoying his hands passing up and down my back and going to a sweet place in my mind. It didn't take much to get me going. I began to caress him, too. His arousal was evident, and we squirmed in each other's arms. I tilted my head back, looking up at his face. We wanted and needed the same thing. "You sure know how to cheer a girl up, Sammy." It was time for an afternoon delight.

Chapter Six
Henniker, New Hampshire, May, 1787

Mary Wallace moved with fluid grace as she carried her sixty-seven-year-old body through her son's magnificent new house. "This is so beautiful, Robert. It's breathtaking."

"I knew you'd like it, Mother, and I couldn't wait to show it to you."

The new structure was two stories tall, farm red with white trim. The solid oak front door led into a vast hall, dominated by a long stairway with a high rail supported by well-turned spindles of white wainscoting enclosing it at the bottom. The look was elegant. The first floor consisted of four large rooms, with entry doors on all four sides of the house. The side doors were enclosed by small mudrooms, reached through French doors with large glass panes in each. The main sitting and dining rooms both featured plastered yellow walls with blue stenciled borders along the top. The massive kitchen's fireplace had an opening eight and a half feet wide. The oven could hold twelve pies for baking. There were six fireplaces in all, four downstairs and two up, and Robert had a den.

Robert and his wife, Jeannette, guided Mary into the dining room, where she admired the large, rectangular dining table, made of solid maple. Eight high backed chairs, made of white pine harvested from his farm, surrounded the table.

"Feel free to sit for a spell, if you need a rest." Robert was always protective of his mother.

"Rest indeed, Robert. We've just begun the tour. I want to see all of it."

See it she did. After completing the downstairs tour, she pushed ahead of her son and daughter-in-law, climbing the stairs with ease, floating upward like a spirit ascending. The four bedrooms were exquisite, two larger and two smaller. Three ran along one side of the house, the large master bedroom was located at the front of the house, and two smaller ones followed in line. The second large room was behind the stairway, toward the rear of the building.

Mary was stunned by the décor in the large back bedroom. Two emerald-green upholstered chairs were placed near a fireplace that shared the flue from the kitchen. The canopy bed at the opposite side was of a solid pine frame. The bedding and canopy were also emerald green.

"I thought you'd like the color scheme, Mother," said Robert. "I know that's your favorite color, it matches your eyes. I did that with a purpose, of course. We're hoping you'll move in with us. This will be your room. You can leave the farm in Londonderry with young James II and live the rest of your days with us. You can be an active participant in your grandchildren's lives as they grow up. We've talked about it, and all agree. We want you here with us. Of course, the choice is yours, but we hope that you'll accept our invitation."

Mary's husband, James, had died of sickness seven years earlier and had left the family farm to his grandson, James II, son of their late son, Thomas. Mary lived at the farm with young James and his family, but she yearned to be closer to her other sons, William and Robert, both of whom had moved to Henniker and started their own orchards. Robert was her favorite, she'd just never been as close to William.

Mary stood still, unable to speak. During the two years this house was being built, she harbored the wish to be included in her son's plans, but was afraid to speak of it.

She didn't want to be presumptuous. A tear trickled down her face.

"Oh, dear Robert, of course I accept. The carriage ride from Londonderry to Henniker is getting to be much too long for me, so visits are more difficult. I'd love to live here in this magnificent house with you." The three people embraced, Robert and Jeannette each planting kisses on Mary's cheek. The final stage of Mary's life would be in Henniker.

A year after Mary came to live with Robert and his family, an unknown visitor approached the house in a carriage on a sunny afternoon. Robert was out in the orchard with his son, and Jeannette was with her daughter, Elaine in the dining room, sewing at the table. Mary heard the carriage approach and peered out the window.

An elderly man in fine apparel brought the carriage to a halt, stepped down and tied the reins to a hitching post in front of the house. Mary waited for him to sound a knock on the front door. "I'll get that, Jeannette."

A tall, well-groomed old man stood on the stone step before the door. Mary stared at the man, trying to recognize him. There was something eerily familiar about him, but her mind was blank, as when trying to recall a dream.

The man stared into Mary's eyes for a moment before speaking. His eyes showed a glaze of moisture. "Are you Mary?" His voice was low, trembling.

"Yes, I'm Mary. Do I know you, sir?" She clasped her hands at her waist, squeezing them.

"No, ma'am. You'd have no way of knowing me, but we've met."

A chill ran through the old woman. "How can that be, sir? What is your name? Perhaps that will give me a clue toward your identity?"

"Ma'am, if I may come inside, I will tell you who I am and why I've traveled here. It's a story that you may find hard to believe, but I swear to you it is true."

Mary was taken by the man's demeanor. He seemed quite sincere, and the emotional timbre of his voice compelled her to learn more about him. Against her better judgment, she stepped back from the door and gestured him in.

His eyes swept the hallway and great stairs above the white wainscoting. The stranger continued to marvel as they entered the sitting room, where Mary gestured him to take a seat in a fine upholstered chair. He eased into it carefully, respectful of its craftsmanship. Mary took a place in a matching chair across from him.

"Now then, please tell me this unbelievable story." Though still puzzled by this man, Mary grew calm and sat comfortably in her chair, anxious to hear the old man's tale.

The gentleman crossed his legs in a relaxed manner and folded his large hands at his waist. "Dear Mary, you were born in no country on this earth, but instead in a ship at sea, one being attacked by pirates. You were born shortly before the pirate captain, having already plundered the ship, was about to leave the vessel and use his ship's cannon to send it to the sea bottom. He was caught by the sound of a baby crying, and he went below decks to investigate. Your father, James, was at your mother's side, along with a midwife, in the Captain's chambers. Your birth, my dear Mary, saved all aboard, for that pirate captain saw in your emerald green eyes the reincarnation of his long-lost love, whose name was Mary."

"That is a very old story, sir, one that I haven't heard since I was small. I thought it was just a parent's way of entertaining a young girl, but as I grew older and came to an age of understanding, they assured me that it was true. They told me that we could talk of it freely, but should not repeat the part about the pirate attack, for that might set fear into people's minds and make family in Ireland unwilling to make a journey to the colonies. So, I know that your story is truth, but how do you know of it?"

"I know because I am that pirate captain, Don Pedro. I am humbly at your service."

Mary braced herself, gripping the armrests of her chair. "You spoke truthfully when you said your story was hard to believe, sir, but I admit I am inclined to believe it. Of course, there were many passengers aboard our ship and all knew of the tale. It has been many years, however, and the people have dispersed throughout New England. Most have probably died by now, and I'm sure different versions of the story have emerged through their families, decades later. Some of the details could have survived, and you might have come across them, helping you to reconstruct the story. There is one further item from the story, however, that we have not discussed, one that was never revealed to others. Only James and I were there when this other issue came up. If you are truly Don Pedro, then you can tell me of it."

The man nodded, closing his eyes for a moment. A tight smile came across his face, and he spoke in a hushed tone. "Dear Mary, it was I who drew a promise from your mother that she give you the name you carry. And there is more. I presented to your mother a gift of fine silk, the same color as your eyes, like my Mary before you. Part of the promise was that she would make your wedding gown of that same emerald silk."

Mary's eyes filled with tears. "It is true, all of it. Only you could know this. Yes, my wedding gown was made of the green silk, as you have said. Mother told me that it was very special. She said she honored the promise as a way of remembering that I, and I alone, was the reason the ship and all aboard were spared. We will preserve that gown for all generations of my family."

Chapter Seven
Wednesday, August 6, 1975, Henniker, New Hampshire

I have to admit that I was impressed with Bart and how much work he had done in a short period of time to get the old house ready. They advertised an open house for Saturday afternoon to kick off the place. They sent out invitations and advertised in the local media as well.

Bart took Sam and me on a brief tour after work. The renovations were completed downstairs so they could start making presentations and allowing tourists. The living quarters upstairs were nearly finished. The three residents moved in.

"Hey, Bart," I called. "You have rather dark, heavy curtains in the dining room. How come? Don't you want to lighten the place up a bit?"

"Heck no, this is a ghost house, remember? I like it dark. It contributes to the atmosphere. Besides, notice the recessed lights in the exposed timbers? They're on a dimmer switch right here." Bart stood in the entry to the dining room from the hallway, fingering the switch. "I can lighten up the room if I want, or adjust as I please."

"So I see," I replied. "I don't know what you've got planned here, but I'm already feeling a sense of spookiness."

Bart was enthusiastic about his new enterprise. He really wanted to make a go of it, despite what others, including myself, thought.

Just as I was starting to think I might enjoy myself this night, Auggie appeared with his mother right beside him.

She was dressed in colonial period clothes, getting right into character.

"Mom," he said, "I'd like you to meet Sam Miller. He's with Martha, whom you already know. This is my mom, Lucy Raymond."

Sam politely walked up to her and gave a gentlemanly handshake. "Nice to meet you, Mrs. Raymond," he said.

"Just call me Lucy. That *Mrs.* stuff reminds me of my dead husband, and I'd just as soon forget him." She scratched her side while talking, as if the costume didn't feel right.

I waved politely from a few feet away, and Lucy returned it, forcing a smile. I was amazed that the old bat still had all her teeth. I turned back to the window and pawed the dark curtain. It was all I could think of to do.

Auggie persuaded Bart to let his mother take the large bedroom in the back, so that one was completed first. The other bedrooms had been freshly plastered, but still needed painting. They decided they might wait until after Saturday's open house, so the smell of fresh paint didn't ruin the air of ghostliness.

Bart and Sam strolled into the sitting room across the hall, with me keeping a few steps behind. Auggie and Lucy eyeballed me and must have felt I was getting too close, so they moved toward the kitchen, keeping to themselves.

"What do you think, Sam?" Bart was eager for constructive feedback.

"You've done a nice job with it. I could live here myself, if you had a good TV antenna on the roof."

Bart slapped Sam on the back. "That's rich. That would sure contribute to the atmosphere. I'm sure Ocean Born Mary watched Johnny Carson after the kids went to bed. No, really, how does it look for what we are trying to do?"

"I'm not exactly sure I know what you are trying to do. I know you are offering tours of the house and will use the Ocean Born Mary legend as a theme, but I'm not that knowledgeable about it. Give me more information."

"Okay Sam, I understand. You're not from around here, so you need to become familiar with the whole thing." Bart shifted gears, talking fast and moving his arms, as if he were drawing it all out on an invisible chalkboard. "We're going to emphasize the ghost idea. You see, Mary still haunts the place. She's been seen over the years, as legend goes, flitting around the house, making weird sounds and scaring the hell out of people. They've even seen her outside at night, a ghostly figure in the night." Bart made a *wooo-oooh* sound as he finished talking.

Sam was expressionless, so Bart tried again. "*Doo-doo-doo-doo, doo-doo-doo-doo,*" he uttered his best *Twilight Zone* theme imitation. Sam was still silent.

"Not so good, eh Sam?" Bart dropped his arms to his side.

"Stick to the first one, Bart. Rod Serling is too contemporary."

"Yeah, you're right. But you get it now, right? The ghost theme, that's what people want to hear about. That's why we have that big round table in the dining room. Auggie and I are thinking about having people gather around the table, doing things to rattle them, maybe even having a séance. Pretty good, don't you think?"

I stepped in close to my two favorite guys. "A séance? Well, don't get ahead of yourself there, brother. Don't forget that a séance can attract the gullible, but it can also bring in skeptics who can't wait to prove it a phony. Maybe you need to go slow. Get a feel for your audience and see how things are going with the tours. Get some publicity going, but don't rush into it."

Bart's face lightened up. "That's good advice. You sound like you're getting interested. We might have a place for you in this, little sister."

"Oh no, hold on there, fella. I'm no shill, and I'm no actress, either. You'd never pull it off with me, even if I wanted to do that, and I don't."

Bart backed off a little. "I get you. But I'll still be interested in your feedback, okay?"

"You'll get that, for sure. You've put a lot of money in this, and I don't want to see you lose your shirt." I was still curious about where Bart got that down payment money. He might be playing with somebody else's shirt.

The show was set for Saturday from two to five o'clock. Sam and I agreed to get there at the start to give Bart and his associates some encouragement. He didn't need us there for the whole open house, but he asked us to be there for the beginning and the end.

It was a warm, sunny day in Henniker. Except for the vapor trail of a jetliner headed for Manchester Airport, the colonial image was pristine from the outside. The house had a lot of charm, especially since the recent refurbishing.

It was set well back off the old road, and the large acreage left plenty of space for parked cars. It wasn't long before people began showing up. Early arrivals are always a good sign.

Sam and I took up a place in the kitchen after greeting Bart and Auggie. Lucy was there with two younger women, who appeared to be in their thirties, and whom I didn't recognize. They were also dressed in colonial clothing. One was tending to something cooking in a large pot on the big wood burning stove. The other was taking wooden bowls out of a cabinet and placing them on the kitchen table. It smelled like a stew. Whatever it was, I knew Lucy hadn't cooked it. She wasn't exactly the domestic type. I don't think she knew her way around a kitchen. *Perhaps that's why her late husband is late,* I thought.

I wasn't interested in introducing myself and Sam to the help. I figured I might never see them again, anyway, knowing Bart's way with women. Lucy forced a hello and went about pretending to be busy, folding towels and scurrying about while achieving nothing visible to the naked eye.

"Say, is that stew for the guests?" asked Sam. I glared at him with a raised eyebrow. "Hey, I'm still hungry," he said in my direction, holding his hands out and shrugging.

"Yes, indeed," said the well-built brunette who stirred the pot. Her colonial-style dress managed to fit very tight in the bodice, showing her twentieth-century charms. "Take a bowl from the table, and I'd be happy to serve you."

Sam smiled at her and gave me a look as he took a bowl and held it out to her with both hands. She ladled some stew into the bowl and gave Sam a smile that indicated she'd be more than happy if he came back for seconds. "I'll just take a seat at the table," said Sam, before he realized that there weren't any chairs there.

"There are picnic tables in the backyard, friend," said the server. "Spoons, too. Why don't you go out and get comfortable?"

Why don't you go to the moon, Alice? I shot in and out of Jackie Gleason mode.

I was following Sam as he headed toward the backdoor when I noticed somebody talking to Bart in the dining room. He was shorter than Bart and heavy set, powerful looking through the neck and shoulders. He wore a gray suit with a dark-blue shirt, but no necktie. Shiny black shoes completed his outfit. If he had been wearing a white tie he wouldn't have looked out of place singing a tune from *Guys and Dolls*.

"I'll catch up with you, Sam. Go enjoy your stew."

Sam nodded and staked out a seat at a table on the back lawn.

I slipped through the kitchen, stuffing my hands into the side pockets of my yellow skirt. I liked having pockets. Don't know why.

The Nathan Detroit character saw me coming, and a smile crossed his face after his eyes worked me over. My skirt was a few inches above the knee, and that seemed to get his attention; my sleeveless, tan, high-neck top gained his favor.

Bart stopped talking when his friend became distracted. Whatever the topic of their discussion, I wasn't to be included in it. I avoided smiling and kept my eyes on Bart.

"Looks like people are starting to show, brother. Are these all invitees?"

"No, some are general public. I think that's a good sign," said Bart. His buddy made a grunt, and Bart got the hint. "Martha, this is Al Martinelli, an old friend from Boston. Al, this is my sister Martha."

Al peered into my eyes. "Nice to meet you, Martha. Bart's told me a lot about you, but he didn't tell me how lovely you are." He gently took hold of my right hand and gripped it with both of his.

I smiled politely. "Did he tell you about my boyfriend, Sam? You'll like him. He's very friendly. He's even got friends in the FBI." I couldn't resist.

He withdrew his hands and folded his arms.

"Al, you don't get up into the country very often, do you?" My eyes examined his outfit.

"No, not too much," he grunted. "But I get around a fair amount."

"What do you do, Al?"

"I'm in finance. I like to work with money."

"I guess you do well. Those are nice looking threads you've got."

He slipped his thumbs under his lapels and ran them down his suit coat. "Yes, well, I like nice things. A man's entitled to live well, don't you agree?"

"Absolutely, Al. Abso-fuckin-lutely." I winked at Bart and poked him in the belly. "I didn't mean to interrupt your talk, Bart. I gotta go mix, see who else has arrived. Nice to meet you, Al."

He nodded, but didn't smile. "The pleasure was all mine, Martha. Hope I'll see you again."

I sauntered across the hall and into the front parlor. A small group was examining a table with various items scattered across it; books, pamphlets, pictures. I lifted one up for a close look. It was a two-page stapled piece with a title, *Ocean Born Mary: A Summary*. There were two small black and white pictures under the title. One, a reproduction of a pencil sketch, showed a woman in a bed with a baby in her arms. She appeared to be in a ship's cabin. The other depicted the ghostly profile of a woman in a long gown, drifting across a forested area.

"Do you approve of it, Martha?" A voice through heavy breath struck my ear.

I turned to see the speaker. It was Auggie.

"I wrote it myself. I did some research at the Henniker Historical Society and the Tucker Library. Got the pictures there, too, with permission to print them, of course. It's for sale, like everything else on the table." He lowered his voice to a whisper. "Fifty cents barely covers the cost of printing, but we have to start churning out some revenue. I figure the pamphlet will give people a quick grounding in the legend, and then we can build on that."

I stepped back and held the paper between us. "That's the right idea, I suppose. Revenue is a good thing. Funny how things always get back to finance. I just met a guy talking to Bart who says that's his line. You know, *finance.*" I made sure to emphasize the final word.

"Yes, that fellow, *Al* something." Auggie lost his enthusiastic look. "I saw him, too. I guess he and Bart go way back."

"Not as far back as you two," I said. "I never heard of the guy myself. What do you know about him?"

Auggie folded his hands and began to tap his thumbs together. "Just that he does work in the financial field, as you said, and that Bart knows him. I guess they've done business before, but not that I've been involved in. Bart has a lot of friends and associates. I don't know all of them."

The refinished hardwood floor clacked as a tall, distinguished looking man approached us. He was trim and had a full head of silver hair. Monty Phillips, the stuffy director of the Henniker Historical Society and part-time History instructor at New Sussex College.

"Hello, young man. So this is what you're up to and why you needed to investigate our collection on Ocean Born Mary. I noticed you there one day, and my associate told me what you were looking for. And I thought you were just going to try to sell pamphlets in the town square at Halloween. This is much more ambitious than I expected." He gazed around the building as he spoke, admiring the refurbished house. "Hello, Martha. Don't tell me you're mixed up in this?"

"Hi, Monty. Always a pleasure." There was a time when I might have made a move on this guy. He was certainly handsome and his frame suggested there was good equipment under those clothes. However, something about his manner held me back. He could be a real turn off.

"Mixed up in it?" My voice almost reached the ceiling. "You say that like there's some sinister plot going on, Monty. No, for what it's worth, this is my brother's gig. Him and Auggie, here."

Monty eased his way around Auggie, eyeing him as if it was an inspection. "I wouldn't say something sinister is going on, but—" He paused for a moment, still checking Auggie up and down. Then his gaze turned to me. If he had X-ray vision, I was naked. "The legend about Mary has been around a long time. She did exist, but the exact truth may never be known. The ghost part, like all ghost stories, is sheer bull. From what I've seen so far, you seem to be leaning in that direction, young man."

"Look friend, ghost stories are part of our culture, and they exist all around the world. They may or may not be real, but they are something that people gobble up because they're fun and entertaining. Who doesn't like a good ghost story? Lighten up, pal, and join the fun. You got something against fun?"

"Not at all. I'm all for a good time, but not at the expense of others. I'll tell you what. I'll take my time looking your enterprise over without judgment. I prefer history over fraud, so I hope you'll show a true interest in historic events and not turn this into a circus sideshow."

I never had liked Auggie, but next to Monty, his stock went up a little.

"Monty, old boy, why don't you take that a step further?" I asked. "What, with your knowledge of history and your work with the Historical Society, maybe you could even offer occasional help. You know, some consultation and advice now and then? If Bart and Auggie make a go of this thing, it will only help the community, you know. What do you say?"

Monty looked at me as if he was caught in a trap. "Which one are you, the Bart or *the Auggie?*" he asked, staring at my brother's partner. He said the *Auggie* as if he were looking at a soiled rag he didn't want to touch.

"Auggie Raymond, nice to meet you." He extended a hand, which hung in the air momentarily.

Monty finally took it for a short shake.

"Monty Phillips."

"Now, that wasn't so hard, was it?" I stepped closer to the men and gave Monty a whack on his firm ass. His eyes almost popped out of his head.

"I might be able to give you some guidance on points of history, *Auggie.* Right now, I'd like to move about, take things in, you see."

Monty made his escape, and Auggie and I stifled our laughter. "That's probably the best action the guy's had in a long time, Martha. You really rattled his cage. I bet you even got some blood flowing below his belt."

"He's just an overstuffed shirt," I said. "But don't underestimate him. He can be a big pain. If he thinks you and Bart are trying to hoodwink the people, he'll be all over you both."

"I get the picture, Martha. I think I'll see how things are going in the kitchen."

"Good." I turned toward the table and continued my inspection. Another pamphlet caught my eye. It showed a drawing of a Y-shaped twig with an explanation of it serving as a dowsing rod. The pamphlet further stated that such a device had been used years ago to try to locate pirate's treasure supposedly buried on the grounds. I know a lot of people believe in the effectiveness of dowsing, but no treasure had ever been found. The pamphlet acknowledged this fact, but also stated that there were over one-hundred and thirty acres on the property, and the grounds were never fully searched. *Auggie and Bart must want to open that door again.*

"You really ought to try that stew, Martha. It's quite good." Sam had satisfied his hunger and found me. "The place is filling up pretty good. Your brother must be very happy."

"If he is, he doesn't show it. Look at that guy he's talking to in the doorway to the dining room. He doesn't look like a barrel of laughs." I pointed back to where I had left Bart and his friend, but they were gone.

"I don't see him," said Sam. "And I didn't see him when I walked through that area a minute ago. I guess they've moved on. Tell me about the guy."

"Bart told me they were friends, but whatever they were talking about, they cut off the conversation as soon as I showed up. I made some brief small talk with the guy.

His name is Al Martinelli and he said he works in finance. I'll bet he does, at the Midnight Savings and Loan. I'll guess Bart is into him for the down payment money on the house."

"Did you ask him?"

"No, but I will. The guy gave me the creeps. I don't like it."

"Bart's a grown man, and he can borrow money from whomever he wishes. Besides, you don't know for certain that this Al somebody is a loan shark. Your best bet is to sit and talk with Bart at a convenient time, but not while this open house is going on. Okay?"

Sam was right. Maybe I had jumped the gun with my assessment of Mr. Martinelli. Maybe he was a legitimate businessman. *And maybe I'm Mary Poppins.*

Chapter Eight
Sunday, August 10, 1975. Henniker, New Hampshire

Lovemaking with Sam never gets old. There isn't a better way to start my day, and this Sunday morning was no different. Sometimes he seems like a schoolboy getting naked with a girl for the first time. He seems embarrassed. At other times, you'd think he invented sex. Either way, I can't get enough of him.

He stayed in bed, falling back to sleep. I decided to grab my shower and slip into cutoff white Levi's and a blue chambray shirt. I rolled my sleeves to the elbow, slipped into old blue tennis shoes and went downstairs, almost skipping a few steps along the way. I wanted to get going.

Bart told me he was going to take some photos of the property, and I knew that meant he'd be out early, when the rising light is best for outdoor photography. I hoped Sam would come, too, but even the aroma of fresh coffee didn't get him moving. Maybe I drained him. *Damn, I'm good.*

Two scrambled eggs with toast and coffee later, there was still no sound from Sam. I scooted up the stairs and made a bathroom trip to brush my teeth, put on a little eye makeup and take care of business. Still no Sam. I left him a note.

I suppose I should have called Bart first, but I decided to head over to his place. *He'll probably be outside and wouldn't get to the phone anyway.* The only one was upstairs. He and Auggie agreed that a phone would be out of place in the downstairs areas that were open to the public.

When I arrived, I saw two figures moving about near the old well that stood to the left of the house out front. It was Bart and Lucy Raymond. He was positioning her on the rope that hung over a pulley above the well. I parked well away along the roadside, so as to not bother them or get in any background.

Bart loved photography and was pretty good at it. He'd managed to get some work published in local newspapers and even contributed some to a book about New Hampshire ski areas. Why he didn't pursue this occupation full time, I never knew. He used it like a hobby that took up time between big schemes.

When he saw me approach, he looked back at Lucy and squeezed off a few quick shots, then told her to take a break. She sighed and strolled over to a wooden chair a few feet away, easing her slow-moving body into it.

"Good morning, Mart, how's your ass?" He sported a black Hasselblad camera on a lanyard around his neck. It reminded me of pictures of astronauts with one dangling near their space suits.

"I've got great news. Should have told you yesterday, but I forgot in all that excitement. I got a story accepted in the *Boston Globe Sunday Magazine*. I sent in a query with a story idea about the house and a couple of pictures. I suggested that they run it soon and a follow up just before Halloween, and they agreed. I'm going to take a bunch of pictures of the place, inside and out, and use Lucy for a human touch, in full colonial garb. I'm going to hit other magazines, too. I'm just getting started."

"Hey, slow down, brother Bart, before you wet yourself. I'm happy for you, but take it easy. Have you got a publicity plan set up?"

"You bet. I'm going to hit all the local papers and magazines, and I'm going to follow up with radio and TV spots. Once I mention the *Globe* publication, they'll take an interest, you can be sure of that. And remember that I told you

I have a contact near Boston who knows a lot about the occult and several groups of followers. I might even make some college lecture appearances talking about the Ocean Born Mary legend. We're off to a pretty good start, wouldn't you say?"

"Yes, I guess so." I had to admit that there was a good turnout at yesterday's event, and the news about getting an article in the *Boston Globe* before Halloween was right on target. But it still wasn't enough to satisfy my uneasiness.

"Yesterday did go well, Bart, and I'm happy for you about that. The *Globe* article sounds great, especially with the timing of it. But I still have my concerns." I was trying to keep from sounding too negative, and what I had to talk to him about might send him crawling into a shell. I had to try, just the same.

"You're always so worried about me, little sister, but there's no need to fret. This plan is going to work just fine, wait and see." Bart caressed the Hasselblad as he spoke, as if he were holding a beloved pet.

"Let's take a walk. There's something I want to talk to you about, in private." I shifted my eyes toward Lucy twice, and Bart got the message. We headed along the yard to the road's edge.

"Okay, Martha, what's on your mind? Let's not make this very long. I don't want Lucy to get her panties in a bunch."

"I know it's none of my business, but I'm concerned about something, and I've got to talk to you about it. Don't get mad at me and please don't misunderstand." I tried to soften up the tone of the conversation, hoping to avoid a storm. Bart nodded.

"Bart, did you pay cash for the down payment, out of your own money, or did you borrow it?"

There was an awkward pause before Bart answered. We kept strolling. "You're right about one thing, Mart, it is none of your business. It's a fair question, a business question, but let me ask one myself first. What should it matter to you? You're not part of the business."

Here we go. Bart should have gone into politics. He often answered a question with a question, a tactic that pols use to avoid an issue. "No, I'm not, but I am part of your family. That's why it matters. I want you to succeed, I really do, but I've seen you get burned before. I don't want to see it happen again. That's all."

Bart smiled and took my hand as we stepped along. "I know your heart's in the right place, kid, and that makes me feel good. But you don't have to worry. I'm a big boy and can take care of myself. I know you don't think much of Auggie, but he's a smart guy and a great partner for me. Don't worry about him."

"I'm always worried about him when he's involved with you. But if you are okay with him and his mom, then I guess I'm okay, too."

Bart stopped and turned toward me, his hands palms up. "There we are, then. All is well." He resumed the walk, heading back to our starting point.

He had almost succeeded in deflecting my first question. "You said before that you put up the down payment, so you didn't borrow anything from Auggie?"

"Nope. Like I said, no need to worry about him."

"So who did you borrow the money from?"

Bart kept walking but his smile went away. "Back to that," he said. Another pause.

"You didn't answer my original question, Bart. Please, I don't mean to pry, but I didn't get to finish."

"Oh, you don't mean to pry? That seems to be exactly what you are doing."

I took a breath, hoping Bart would calm down. I decided to try an end run. "Tell me about that guy yesterday, you know, Al Martinelli. I think he liked me."

Bart glared at me for a moment. He knew I was on target. "He certainly liked you, sister. He's not exactly Cary

Grant, but he loves to charm the ladies and throw his money around. That's about the extent of his charm. I can set you up on a date if that's what you'd like."

"That's not what I was curious about. Sam's all I can handle; all I want to handle, for that matter. I was wondering if you have done business with him before. How did it go?"

"I've always done well with Al. Of course, I've only done business with him a couple of times, nothing big or exciting. He's very good with finance."

"I thought you and Auggie were sixty-forty partners in this, so does Al own a piece of it, too?"

"Absolutely not. Sorry, I didn't mean to snap at you. Okay, I took out a loan from Al, but I backed it up with my own collateral. I told you I have assets. This way I don't reduce my cash. It's good business. Does that satisfy your curiosity?"

It didn't, but I couldn't say that to Bart. I understood his business logic, a very common practice. I preferred, however, that he borrow money from a bank, not some loan shark. That part still had me worried.

When I got back to my apartment, Sam was up and dressed, reading the newspaper at the kitchen table. A cup of coffee filled the air with a nice aroma. But I wasn't feeling nice.

"Sam, I need your help."

He looked up from his newspaper, his eyes focused on my face. I liked that. He always paid attention when I spoke to him. "What have you got in mind? I'm always glad to help you."

"It's that guy Al Martinelli, Bart's buddy in the finance world. I have a bad feeling about him. Bart took out a loan from him and it worries me. I just talked to him and I feel like he's holding something back. I need to know if Martinelli is legit."

Sam nodded. "You think he's not the kind of person Bart should be doing business with, is that it?"

"Damned right, but I don't know how to go about checking him out. He's from Boston, so I doubt that Chief Powers will know about him. I wonder if your friend Eli might be able to dig into it for us, what with his contacts and all. Could you call him and ask for help? Maybe he can at least tell us where to look."

Sam scratched his chin. "I suppose he might be able to do that. I'll give him a call. Those guys have access to databases with information about all kinds of people. Maybe he can give us something."

I didn't know if this track would get me anywhere, but I felt better knowing Sam had Eli to contact.

Chapter Nine
Henniker, New Hampshire, February 13, 1814

Robert Wallace stood next to his mother's bed, a fire crackling in the bedroom fireplace, doing its best to warm the sickly old Mary. Her eyes were faint, and her lids closed every few seconds, opening when she made an attempt at speech. Robert was at her right side, clutching her chilled hand. There was little time left.

Mary Wallace was ninety-four years old and had been in poor health for weeks. Her breathing was short and labored, and she coughed frequently with the deep, rumbling sound of congestion. A howling snowstorm whipped at the house. There was no way to fetch the local doctor or to summon Robert's brother.

Robert's wife, Jeanette Wallace, stood at the foot of the great bed as death prepared to enter the room. The old woman lay propped against two large down pillows, her mouth open, gasping for each breath as her moments ticked down.

"Robert, my dear, you must promise me something." Mary's voice could barely be heard, and her son bent down close to her head. He tapped on her hand in acknowledgement. "I know you and your brother, William, have never been close, but I hope you will make an effort to be friends. I've had a fine and happy life, for the most part. Your father was a great man and brought me much happiness. I am ready to leave this world without regret. My only wish is that you and William can live in harmony and keep the Wallace family close." She did her best to turn her head toward Robert and gaze into his eyes.

"I promise you, Mother, that I'll make every effort to do as you say." Robert smiled and gripped his mother's hand, feeling what little life was left in it. He looked back at Jeanette without speaking. Tears were showing in her eyes.

Robert's head jerked toward his mother when he thought he heard a groan. Her face seemed to stiffen with her mouth still opened, and Robert felt her hand become lifeless. Ocean Born Mary was gone from this world.

Jeanette gathered close to Robert and bade farewell to Mary. Their sadness filled the room. "Oh Robert," said Jeanette. "I'm going to miss her so much. I can't believe that she's gone."

Robert faced his wife standing beside the bed. He wrapped his arms around her. "True, my dear, she has left us. But I feel that the spirit of Ocean Born Mary Wallace will always be here."

It was an unusually warm day in January. The usually snow-covered ground in Henniker was bare. There was no whiteness to the hills, and Robert Wallace felt alive with unseasonable energy.

"Jeanette, I'm going to take a ride into town." Robert's voice carried up the front stairway to his wife, who was changing the bedding in their room.

"Very well, dear, but be home in time for dinner," she replied.

Robert trotted out to the barn behind the house and saddled his horse. In a moment, he was galloping his mount along Bear Hill Road, looking forward to meeting up with townsfolk for some talk and news of the day, an experience rarely enjoyed in January under such warm and sunny conditions.

Less than a mile away from home, the enjoyment of the day was stolen. Robert's horse pulled to a sharp halt. It reared up, whinnying in fear. A black bear growled from a spot behind a nearby tree. Startled by the sound of the horse, it too reacted in fear and sped away, deeper into the woods.

Robert pulled back on the reins, trying to calm his mount, but the horse resisted, rearing up with great force once more. Robert struggled to regain control of the reins. His grip grew slippery. His seat upon the mount became unsteady. He was thrown backward off the horse, which raced away, retracing his route home. Its rider lay sprawled on the ground, his head smashed on a boulder beside the road.

Robert lay motionless, barely alive. His eyes dimmed as he struggled to utter the words, "Mother, Mother." The unusually warm January air gave way to a sudden, frigid breeze crossing his face, like a caress from a gentle hand. Less than a year after the loss of his mother, Ocean Born Mary, Robert Wallace was dead.

Having inherited the great Wallace house in Henniker from his father, Robert Jr. and his wife moved in soon after his father's death. His mother, Jeanette, moved into the guest room previously occupied by her mother-in-law, and Robert Jr. took the master bedroom. Since they had no children, one of the rooms was opened as guest quarters.

The farm continued to prosper under Robert Jr.'s leadership, for he was a bright and well-educated man. The family still held businesses in Londonderry, which added to their affluence. A large flax farm had begun to prosper under Wallace, and it played a major part of the success of the linen industry in Londonderry.

It was common for Robert to make trips to Londonderry. He stayed overnight, in quarters behind a barn, that had been added by his father. It was a small cabin with a living and cooking area and a private bedroom. The main house was occupied by the hired manager of the farm and his family. The manager's wife saw to the maintenance of the Wallace visiting quarters.

Two decades of prosperity followed for Robert. His orchards and flax business brought him wealth and notoriety. He employed many workers, making him very well liked and appreciated among the townsfolk in both Henniker and Londonderry. But his life felt incomplete.

At first, his childless marriage didn't bother him. He worked long hours and traveled often. But as the years went on, he believed that his wife was barren and nothing could be done.

Robert was into his forties when he first saw her. He was on a trip to Londonderry and rode up to his quarters at the farm in a carriage drawn by a single horse. He left several articles of clothing in Londonderry and needed only one garment bag for travel. He drew the bag from the carriage and turned to find a servant man approaching, his slightly graying hair being blown by a breeze.

"Good day, Mr. Wallace, you're a bit early today." The sun was not very high in the June sky.

"Hello, Andrew, how good to see you. Yes, I left Henniker yesterday and spent the evening in Manchester. I left there rather early today. It feels good, as always, to arrive at the farm. I'll never tire of the place."

"Let me take your bag, sir." Andrew reached for the sole piece of luggage, and Robert released it. "A worker has been assigned to maintain your quarters, sir. She is inside getting it ready for you. I'm sorry for the inconvenience."

"Not to worry," said Robert. "Why don't you introduce me, and then I'll walk around a bit?" Robert's head spun about, taking in the lovely view of the acres before him.

Andrew smiled with a nod and led the way into the small building.

Once inside the cabin, Robert was immediately taken by the pretty young woman, whom he guessed was about eighteen years old. Her light hair pleased him, it seemed appropriate for a fair young lady working at a flax farm.

The young woman was finishing sweeping the floor when she heard the men enter. She turned to face them, holding her broom at her side.

"Ruth Ann Winslow, this is your employer, Mr. Robert Wallace." Andrew's tone was soft, but direct.

"Oh my, hello, Mr. Wallace," she greeted him with a trembling voice. "I'm sorry that I didn't complete preparing your quarters before your arrival."

Robert stared at her momentarily. "That's perfectly all right, Miss Winslow. It's really my fault for being early. Think nothing of it." His eyes traveled up and down her figure and returned to her smooth complexion and deep blue eyes.

Andrew carried Robert's bag into the bedroom and laid it on a stand under a window. When he returned to the main room, Robert had moved closer to Ruth Ann. He turned toward the servant.

"Thank you, Andrew. That will be all."

"Very well, sir," said Andrew. "Come along now, Ruth."

"That's all right, Andrew. I'd like her to stay a moment while I ask her a few questions. She'll be along shortly."

Andrew nodded and strode away, leaving his employer to question the help.

Robert waited until Andrew was gone before facing Ruth Ann. When he did, his admiring look was not lost on the young servant woman. As he removed his topcoat, he felt that he had sent a bad message to her.

"Don't look so alarmed, young lady. I'm just taking off this dusty thing. Perhaps I should shake it off outside. I don't want to make your work any harder." Robert stepped outside the door and removed his coat, giving it a flap in the air to get rid of the road dust. He folded it over his arm and reentered the cabin. Ruth Ann was standing in the same spot as before.

"How long have you been working here, Ruth? I trust you live nearby with your parents, perhaps?" Robert folded his hands at his waist, smiling at his new acquaintance.

"I've worked at your farm for a few years now, as my parents have also. They both work at growing and harvesting the flax. They also thresh and ret the crop." And then Robert stopped her rapid explanation.

"I get the picture. Tell me, do you prefer to be called Ruth or Ruth Ann?"

"Either one is fine, sir." Her hands clung tightly to the broom.

Robert let out a laugh and shook his head. "Very well, then. I'll use both, but I think I'll use Ruth Ann most frequently. It has an elegance to it. And do you and your parents live in Londonderry?"

"Yes, sir, we have a small house on the edge of town."

"I'm pleased that you are all working here. I hope that will continue." Robert gazed around the room. "You've done a fine job here, Ruth Ann, and I'm very pleased to have met you."

"Thank you, sir. I'll be cleaning it every day while you're here."

"That's good, Ruth Ann. I'll be out and about by eight o'clock every morning, so you can make your schedule accordingly. Oh, and please call me Robert, won't you?" He leaned forward at the waist, waiting for an answer.

"Yes, sir—ah, Robert. I will." She giggled, bringing a hand to her mouth.

"Good. You should run along now. I don't want to keep you from your other tasks. Don't worry any further about the floor. It looks fine."

"Very well, sir. Robert. It's a pleasure to meet you." The young woman scurried out the door, closing it softly behind her.

The next morning, Robert was out of the cabin before Ruth Ann showed up to perform her duties. He went about the farm, checking on all its enterprises and meeting with his manager. Throughout the day, however, his thoughts kept falling to young Ruth Ann.

Chapter Ten
Londonderry, New Hampshire, September, 1834

Robert Wallace expanded his flax crop that year, planting additional acreage in the spring. It was nearly ready for harvest by late summer, in time for his workers to cut the flax plants, remove the seeds and spread the plants in an open field for several weeks. He needed more workers. That gave Robert a convenient excuse for making more trips to the farm and staying longer.

His affair with Ruth Ann Winslow began slowly. He didn't want to make his attraction to her obvious. Upon the second day after meeting her, he avoided direct contact, but couldn't keep her out of his thoughts the entire day. By the third day, he had to see her. He delayed leaving his cabin until she arrived to perform her housekeeping tasks. To his pleasure, the attraction was mutual, and soon they were in each other's arms, kissing and caressing one another. They became lovers.

Robert was sitting at the small table near the cooking stove one clear, September morning, awaiting Ruth Ann's arrival. As was often the case, he made excuses for delaying the start of his work day. He knew Andrew had figured out the deception, but he was confident that his servant would keep a discreet tongue. When Ruth Ann entered the cabin, Robert rushed from the table to take his prize in an embrace. In an instant they were on the bed making love.

He cleansed himself at a wash basin before dressing and heard Ruth Ann's voice behind him. "Dear Robert, the weeks have flown by, and I fear that winter will be upon us too soon. What will we do then? I can't bear the thought of the harshness of winter keeping us apart."

"I feel the same way, my love, but there is not much that can be done. Winter is beyond our control. We'll have the spring to look forward to. Besides, we have many weeks of fall to enjoy being together. All of the crops will be ready for harvest, and I'll come here often."

Robert completed dressing and looked at his lover. Her face showed the disappointment of a woman who was caught in the trap of being a mistress. He approached her and took her chin in his hand as she sat on the edge of the bed. "We must enjoy each day we are together, my dear. I must leave for home this afternoon, but shall be back in two weeks, I promise." He kissed her on the lips and was quickly out the door.

Robert had discovered an idyllic situation. Although he still loved his wife, Ruth Ann brought a new excitement to his life. His sexual energy was renewed, and the infrequency of lovemaking at home no longer tore at him. Ruth Ann was a wish come true, bringing him a satisfaction that he'd previously feared was gone from his life.

Robert stoked the fire in the stove, adding wood to heat the cabin on a cold, mid-November morning. He had arrived in the middle of the previous day, but saw no sign of Ruth Ann. Awaiting her appearance this morning filled him with anticipation, and he prepared the cabin for their time together. He remained in his night shirt.

As usual, she did not knock before entering, and she found Robert lying across the bed, covers pulled up to his chest.

"At last, my dear Ruth Ann, we are together again. Two weeks away from you since my last visit has been almost unbearable. Undress quickly, dear, and come by my side."

Without speaking, she did as requested, and the two made love. Robert's passion seemed to far exceed Ruth

Ann's, but it didn't bother him. His lust blinded him from her mood. When they had finished, Robert fell back against the pillows, and he snuggled close to his lover. She was still silent.

Robert drifted off to a light sleep, content and peaceful. His rest was interrupted, however, by the sound of retching. Through squinting eyes, he saw Ruth Ann across the room, bent naked over the stand, which held a wash basin.

He rushed out of bed and drew close to her, unsure whether to touch her. He overcame his reluctance to make contact and began slowly rubbing her back as she vomited into the basin. He shot back to bed.

Saying nothing, Robert cleansed himself in the main room before dressing. He didn't know what to make of Ruth Ann's condition. When she had finished, he took the basin to the outhouse to dump its contents. Once in the cabin, he rinsed it with fresh water from a pitcher and tossed the liquid out the bedroom window. Ruth Ann was dressed by the time he had completed his tasks of heating fresh water on the stove, washing his face and shaving.

As Robert heated water for tea, Ruth Ann emerged into the main room, fully dressed and looking pale as a ghost. He went to her and clutched her shoulders gently. "What sickness has taken you, my dear? Here, take a seat."

He motioned to a chair at the table, but Ruth Ann shook her head. "No, I'm all right, Robert. It has passed. I'll be fine."

"Perhaps I should take you to town to see the doctor."

"No, dear Robert, that won't be necessary. I've already seen the doctor."

Robert's face was blank with the ignorance of a man who had no knowledge of the early stages of a woman's pregnancy. "You've seen the doctor? Tell me then, Ruth Ann, what is it? You have me frightened."

By the time she had explained her pregnancy to Robert, he was sitting in a chair, his face more pale than hers, and she was standing. Being childless, Robert and his wife had never gone through the experience of morning sickness.

In the spring of 1835, a beautiful girl baby was born to Ruth Ann Winslow in Londonderry. Robert had faced her parents and explained himself to them, assuring them that it was he who had taken advantage of their daughter. He asked them to help him keep word of the affair away from the people of Henniker. In return for their silence, he promised that they would always have employment on his farm, and that he would make sure there was no financial burden placed on them or Ruth Ann.

When Robert was first able to visit the child, he was taken by her beauty and the fact that he had, at last, produced an offspring. He loved the child dearly. He promised Ruth Ann that he would make sure the child, named Sarah, would be well educated, so that she might lead a life among the privileged class and marry into it. When Sarah reached the appropriate age, she was sent off to boarding school in Wellesley, Massachusetts. Robert paid all the bills, but insisted that all correspondence be sent to Ruth Ann's address in Londonderry.

Ruth Ann was grateful for Robert's kindness, but feared that all financial help would stop if something happened to him. She decided to keep all correspondence and receipts from the school, providing a record of her attendance and that the bills were paid for by Robert Wallace Jr. She hoped that this record would provide Sarah a means of receiving an inheritance upon his passing. It would be the only way she could provide for her daughter, unless Robert would take it upon himself to include his only child in his will.

Sarah grew into a tall and beautiful woman, with light hair and emerald green eyes, much like those of the great grandmother she never knew. When Sarah was old enough to understand, her mother told Sarah about the connection to the Wallace family in Henniker and of Ocean Born Mary, whose story was often told in Londonderry. Sarah learned to keep quiet about her bloodline until such a time as necessary.

Chapter Eleven
Friday, September 5, 1975, Henniker, New Hampshire

Sam and I decided to ride out to see Bart after work and congratulate him on the article that had just run in the *Boston Globe Sunday Magazine*. It told the story of Ocean Born Mary in condensed form and had three pictures of the house taken by Bart, one an exterior shot and two inside. It was great publicity.

Bart and Auggie were ecstatic about the *Globe* article and expected an increase in house tour attendance this weekend. Although they had completed the renovations to the house, they still kept the upstairs off limits. If the visitors inquired heavily enough about the second-floor rooms, they could always change their minds. If something pays, you go with it.

Sam met me at my place, and we drove over in my car after a quick dinner. We still had over an hour of daylight ahead of us. I loved dusk during the fall. Despite all that had happened the year before, Henniker was still a peaceful little town, although the college kids would soon be arriving to end the summer quiet.

As we drove across town, I asked Sam if his call to Eli had been productive.

"I'm afraid not," said Sam. "He talked to a contact at the FBI who deals with RICO cases."

"What?"

"RICO. Ready for this: it stands for Racketeer Influenced and Corrupt Organizations Act. Just think Mafia.

Anyway, his guy couldn't find anything on anyone named Al Martinelli. That means one of two things."

I stared at Sam.

"Either he's never been caught at whatever he does, or—you're not going to like this."

I kept staring.

"He's an upstanding, clean as a whistle business man."

"You're right, I don't like that possibility. I'll go with the first one."

Sam shook his head. "Just because he looks like he walked off the set of *The Godfather* doesn't mean anything. Maybe he's just a living stereotype. I don't think you should lose sleep over him."

"Just the same, I don't trust him."

When we arrived, I saw a sign posted beside the walkway to the front door. It gave the tour hours: *Saturday and Sunday beginning 10:00 a.m. to 5:00 p.m. on the hour. Wed. Fri. 2:00 to 5:00 p.m. Tours approximately 45 mins.*

We entered without knocking, and Bart's voice called out from the kitchen. "Who's there?"

"Just me and Sam, brother."

"In the kitchen. Come on in."

Bart, Auggie and Lucy were gathered at the kitchen table, chomping on grinders from the Henniker Market, with glasses of bourbon close by. There was the pungent smell of raw onions, tuna fish and Italian cold cuts. White butcher paper lay sprawled over the table. Auggie and Lucy gnawed at their food without looking up. Bart put his down and greeted us, talking through a mouth half full of grinder.

"Pardon me if I don't shake hands," he said, clutching his meal. "Did you guys eat yet?"

I waved off the idea of food, not sure if he was going to give up half of his. "Yes, we've had dinner, but thanks anyway."

"What brings you around, Mart?"

"Just wanted to see how things are going along. You three seem settled in pretty well. I like the sign out front. It shows that you're really open for business."

"That was Auggie's idea," Bart said, nodding to his partner, who raised one hand while eating. "I made it up with stencil lettering. We need some organization to the tour sessions. Auggie and I will conduct the tours and now that business is picking up, we'll hire some part timers to help with the ticket sales and gift shop stuff."

"Are those part timers the ones we met at the open house?" I asked.

"Yeah, those gals are pretty good."

"I'm sure they are." Before he could respond, I changed the subject. "Aren't you going to have any night hours? That would seem better for ghost stuff."

"We're thinking about it," Auggie chimed in. "Certainly, Halloween's going to be a big night. We might hold some other special events at night, too. We'll see."

Sam ambled around the room, straying over to the old wood stove. Cast iron pots and pans hung from hooks above it. They were antiques, adding to the atmosphere. A wooden block with cutlery was on a service table beside the stove.

"How about Lucy?" I asked. "What's her role going to be?"

She put her grinder down and handled the question herself. "I'm going to add atmosphere, so to speak, while keeping an eye on the money at the same time. You know how some hired help can be at times. We don't want anybody trying to get slick with the cash." She went back to her dinner, satisfied with her explanation of her duties.

That's the Lucy I knew, always interested in cash and its whereabouts. I wondered who would be keeping an eye on her. She'd probably have deep pockets sewn into that bulky colonial costume.

Our conversation was interrupted by the sound of a car pulling up to the house. "I'll check out the visitor," I said as the others put down their food and hastened to wipe their hands on napkins, as if they sensed someone important. Sam tapped his fingers on the stove and followed me at a distance.

"Holy cow," I called out from the front door back into the house. "Come get a look at this."

I heard the noise of people scrambling out of chairs, followed by footsteps on the wooden floor. They were at me in a second, crowding the open doorway. We stood silent as we gaped at the image before us.

A tall, slender woman came gliding up the walkway to the house carrying a handbag at her side. Her graceful walk showed maturity, but her age was hard to guess. She had long, red hair and wore a yellow, loose fitting skirt below the knee, and a long-sleeved, ruffled white blouse that was buttoned to the neck.

As she approached, I studied Sam, and he returned the look at me. The woman's eyes were a deep green shade, the kind that I imagined when I read about Ocean Born Mary. I looked at Bart. "Anyone you know, Bart?" He never answered, but kept his gaze fixed on the image approaching. She seemed to be drifting along with the breeze. My mouth felt dry.

She eyed the sign in the yard as she passed it, stopping at last before the group clustered in the opened front doorway. "Hello, I'm looking for Bart Sanborn." Her voice was strong, in contrast to the lithe image she presented.

Bart cleared his throat, stepping forward as the rest of us stepped aside. "At your service, ma'am. How can I help you?"

Bart looked as though he were caught in a dream.

I didn't know what to make of her. *What is happening? Is she real? Is she an actress playing a part? Does she know whom she looks like?*

"Mr. Sanborn, may I come in? I have a story that you must hear." The tall woman placed a foot on the threshold, as if she already had her answer. *She might float like a feather, but she's got some nads.*

Without words, we spread away from the door, like the Red Sea parting for Moses, and this elegant figure of a woman made her entrance. There was a quiet around us. Even her footsteps made no sound.

Bart motioned to the dining room. "Let's take places in the dining room, at the large table. There's room for all of us there."

"All of us?" questioned the visitor. "If you're the proprietor of the business, as I gathered from the recent newspaper article, you're the one I need to address, Mr. Sanborn."

Bart overcame his dreaminess momentarily. "These people are family, friends and business associates. They could all be affected by your story. Please, have a seat."

"Very well, Mr. Sanborn, if that's what you want."

I peeked at Sam and gave a quick shake of my hand at my waist, like Ed Norton giving Ralph Cramden the *sheesh* sign. Fortunately, the sound of chairs scraping the floor muffled Sam's giggle. We settled in and placed our folded hands on the table in unison, as if a service were about to start.

Sitting as straight as a tree, the woman took the lead. "I'll start by introducing myself. My name is Teresa Thurgood. I'm currently from Boston, but was originally from Londonderry. Other than Mr. Sanborn, I don't know any other names, so would you please indulge me?"

"I'll be happy to, Miss—excuse me, is it Miss or Mrs.?"

"Please, call me Teresa. I prefer to be informal and, no, I'm not married."

"Very well, Teresa," said Bart before going around the table making introductions. He followed with an offer of a beverage, and Teresa agreed to a glass of water. Bart, Auggie and Lucy took a moment to fetch the drinks they had already poured for themselves in the kitchen. Sam accepted a bourbon, neat, while I declined. I sensed something substantial was about to happen, and I wanted to keep a clear head.

"Now that we are all comfortable, Teresa, it's time for you to begin your story," said Bart. "I'm very anxious to hear it, whatever it may be." Bart drifted back into his dream state as he gazed at this beautiful woman with emerald eyes.

I inspected Auggie and Lucy's faces, too. They were not in a dream. I saw suspicion on both. Auggie untwined his fingers, while his mother sat very still, continuing to size up the visitor.

Teresa cleared her throat, took a sip of water and sat with hands in her lap. "I'm sure my name means nothing to any of you, but my lineage should." She stiffened slightly. "I am a direct descendant of Mary Wallace. She is my great, great, great, great, great grandmother." Teresa paused, letting the impact of her claim set in. Almost on cue, Bart, Auggie, and Lucy grabbed their glasses and swallowed bourbon. Sam and I just stared at her, his lips closed, while mine were opened in a tight smile. I knew this was going to be good.

Auggie spoke first. "Look, Miss Thurgood, we didn't just fall off the pumpkin truck. Bart and I have done a great deal of research before starting this business. Hell, we grew up around here and have heard a great deal about Ocean Born Mary. I've spent a fair amount of time at the Henniker Historical Society recently and don't recall coming across the name Thurgood in Mary's story. You're making a wild claim, so I hope you can offer proof."

Lucy nodded agreement at her son.

"I know I'm dropping a bombshell on you and, yes, I can offer proof of my lineage." Teresa lifted her handbag and placed it on the table, undoing the clasp and reaching inside. She removed a folder and opened it.

"I'm not at all surprised that you don't know of my side of the family," said Teresa. "There's good reason for that. I'm sure you know of Mary's son, Robert, and his son, Robert, Jr., both of whom owned this grand house? You certainly also know that Robert, Jr. had no children."

"That's correct," said Bart. "He was the last Wallace to own this house, and he is the last of her lineage that anyone can trace. The records of females are clouded at best and there doesn't seem to be anyone after Robert, Jr."

Auggie's brow was wrinkled, unsure what was coming next. Lucy's hands had become clenched.

Sam's gentle voice prevented the discussion from getting heated. "Teresa, are you making a claim on this property? Is that why you're here?"

She turned her head to Sam, appearing soothed by his voice. "No, I'm not. My family story has been kept buried intentionally. Let me tell you that story before you come to any conclusions. Please, let me proceed."

Sam's question and her answer worked like a sedative to the others, calming the growing tension in the room. Bart sipped more bourbon, and the others did the same.

"Robert Wallace, Jr. did not have any children that anyone knew of. Though he grew up in Henniker, he took many trips to Londonderry, where his family had established very successful businesses and owned considerable land."

"Yeah, yeah," said Auggie. "Tell us something we don't know."

Teresa looked directly at Auggie, readying her counter punch. "Robert Wallace, Jr. had a long-lasting affair with a young woman who worked for him in Londonderry. Her name was Ruth Ann Winslow. When Ruth Ann got pregnant by Robert, he made a deal with her parents to always provide employment for them and to ensure that the child would receive an education and be properly cared for, as long as they never revealed the identity of her father. The child was Sarah Winslow."

That sounded quite possible to me, and Teresa told the tale without the slightest quiver in her voice. I saw no reason, as yet, not to believe her. Bart also looked like he was accepting the story, but Auggie and Lucy were not convinced.

"This still sounds like a fishy tale to me, and anybody could have thought it up," said Auggie.

Teresa continued. "Sarah was sent to the Fitzgerald Hall School in Massachusetts, with Robert paying all of her bills. But, to help maintain the secret, he had all the receipts and correspondence sent to Ruth Ann's address in Londonderry. As Robert was getting along in years, Ruth Ann Winslow feared that he might pass on and leave nothing to their daughter, so she kept all the receipts—signed by Robert Wallace Jr.—as proof of Sarah's lineage. I have photocopies of them here in my folder." Teresa pushed the papers to Sam for inspection, and he sent them around the table.

"That's not official proof of anything," squawked Auggie.

"No, it isn't," returned Sam. "But I don't think it takes a genius to see a true connection. Why would Robert Wallace Jr. sign off on bills paid to the Fitzgerald School for a child other than his own?"

"Well, why didn't this secret family ever cash in before? The Wallaces were a rich bunch."

"Yes, Auggie, they were rich," answered Teresa. "But so were the Winslows, in a way. They were rich in pride and dignity and never tried to *cash in,* as you say. They were honest and proud people, and decided to keep the secret."

I was starting to like this gal more and more. Her manner was gentle but firm, and her physical appearance was consistent with the written descriptions of Ocean Born Mary. It's pretty hard to fake the height, the hair and the emerald eyes, unless she was a master of disguise. I was sold.

"You say you're not trying to grab a piece of this property," spoke Lucy. "Then just what do you want? Why are you breaking family tradition?"

The more I liked Teresa, the less I liked Lucy.

"That's a fair question," said Teresa. "I don't mind. The simple truth is that I haven't had a comfortable life. I'm unmarried, having failed in marriage before. I had been receiving a small alimony until my husband died several years ago. When I read about this business, I decided to contact Bart and offer myself to be part of the story of Ocean Born Mary, which, after all, I truly am. I only ask for a fair wage for work performed in the house. I'll take up residence elsewhere. That's all I ask. I'll leave it to all of you in the business to decide if I'm worth hiring."

I grinned at Sam and gripped his hand on the table. He was with me. Auggie and Lucy fell silent.

Bart looked down for a moment. When he had composed his thoughts, he asked for clarification. "So, you don't want any share of our business, just a job here at the house, is that correct? You can call me Bart."

"Yes, Bart, that's right. It's all well and good to have Lucy pose for pictures wearing colonial dress, but here you have a chance to have a direct descendent of Mary Wallace actually working here. There must be a variety of ways to work with that. I could conduct tours and speak to the people, or even just work in the gift shop, whatever you think best. I'm sure I'll be good for business."

"Hold on there, just hold on," Auggie shouted. "You guys sound like you're buying this story—lock, stock and barrel—without any further checking." He glared at Teresa. "I hope you won't be offended, Miss Thurgood, if I want to get more verification."

Auggie could always get under my skin without much effort. "Where are you going to get this verification, Auggie? She has explained to us that her family kept this relationship to the Wallace family a secret. I don't think you're going to find another paper trail."

"I don't know, but I'd like to at least try before we cut her in on the business."

"That's all right, Martha," said Teresa. "It's a fair position for Auggie to take. But I said I don't want a share of the business, just a job. I need the income and feel it would be fun work. I hope you won't make me wait a great while."

The room went quiet for a moment before Bart spoke up. "There won't be any need for you to wait, Teresa. We can put you on provisionally while Auggie checks out your story. You can start tomorrow. It will be a low-profile position, to start. You can help with the ticket and gift sales, and I'll train you myself, not to put a burden on Lucy. Tours don't start until ten o'clock, so if you come in at eight, there'll be plenty of time to break you in on what we are doing."

Auggie grumbled, and Lucy looked as though she were going to spit.

"As the majority owner, the hiring is my decision to make," said Bart. "So, we'll start you at minimum wage and see how it goes for a two-week trial. Surely that will give you enough time, Auggie." Bart spoke without taking his eyes off Teresa.

I was proud to see my brother stand up to Auggie, pulling rank on him. *Amazing how the power of a beautiful woman can move a guy.*

"Very well," said Auggie. "A two-week trial it is. As you suggest, Bart, we'll see what happens after that."

Chapter Twelve
Late April, 1931, Henniker, New Hampshire

Allan Royston struggled to make a living with writing and photography, for he was more adept at the latter than the former. His mother, Abigail, lived with her forty-five-year-old son in the house he had purchased six years earlier, and they had some success at resurrecting the legend of the house haunted by the ghost of the woman born at sea and spared by a ruthless pirate. But the Great Depression came. It caused a drop in attendance at the tours he conducted at the grand old Ocean Born Mary house. He had to spark new interest.

"Be sure to clean up the parlor, Mother, before the reporter arrives," said Allan, standing next to his elderly mother in the kitchen. "I have to go upstairs and select some of my pictures to show him."

Abigail Royston kept a low fire going in the stove for making tea. "Don't worry, son, I'll take care of it. It's so exciting that you were able to get a newspaper reporter all the way from Nashua. A new story in the paper will surely help business."

The two went about their tasks, eager for the arrival of the reporter. Allan had tried in vain to stir interest in the Concord newspaper recently. He hoped this would be the shot in the arm his venture desperately needed.

A black Chevrolet sedan rumbled to a stop along the road in front of the house, and the noise sent Allan rushing to the bedroom window. A small young man, perhaps in his late twenties, emerged from the car. He wore a brown three-piece suit with matching shoes, and a fedora hat that seemed to swallow his head. He carried a small briefcase at his side. Allan scrambled to gather a collection of photographs, which were spread out on his bed. He scooped them into a folder and rushed down the stairs.

Allan took a place in the parlor with his folder near him, letting his mother answer the knock at the door. She greeted the young man, introduced herself and brought him to meet Allan. "David Robertson, from the Nashua Post," said the reporter, extending a hand to his host. Allan took the hand for a brief shake and pointed to an upholstered chair across from his own. The two got down to business.

"This is a marvelous house, Mr. Royston. I've heard a great deal about it and am thrilled that my editor allowed me to work on this story."

"Thank you, young man. Let me tell you why I contacted your paper."

Mr. Robertson pulled a notepad from his briefcase and slipped a pencil from his shirt pocket. The eager young reporter was just what Allan had hoped for, rather than someone who had heard stories of Ocean Born Mary for decades.

"David, just a few weeks ago, I was sitting in the very chair that I'm in now. Mother had retired for the evening and was upstairs in her room. I had a small fire going to take the chill out of the cold spring air." Allan pointed to the old fireplace in the parlor. "The crackling of the fire was all I could hear, but I happened to look up for some reason that I can't explain. I got up and moved to where I could see through the doorway into the front hall. It was an incredible sight."

Robertson pushed his pencil across his pad with haste, trying to capture Allan's every word.

"I saw a tall, female figure with long, reddish hair descending the stairs. She wore a loose gown that seemed to float around her, and her hair ruffled about her as if a gentle wind were teasing it. I didn't know what to make of it." Allan paused to let his guest catch up with his notes.

"She continued down the stairs, while I remained frozen in place in the hall. The front door opened by itself, and the figure drifted out into the yard. Overcoming my paralysis, I followed her. The moon was full, and I had an excellent view in the night. I chased after her as she circled the house toward the back and disappeared into the orchard. Her movement was swift. I couldn't keep up with her, and in a moment, she was gone. I rushed into the orchard, but there was no trace of her."

"That's astonishing, Mr. Royston. You're certain that the moon was full?" asked Robertson, trying to sound like the diligent reporter.

"Absolutely, young man. It was earlier this month, so you can check that out in the almanac."

"Of course, sir. Go on, please."

"I was away from the house the next night, but when I returned, I saw her again. She was standing in the upstairs front window, staring out. I moved carefully inside and removed my shoes before coming in. I made my way upstairs and searched for her, but to no avail. On the third night, I was the one looking out a window. I had prepared my camera with a flash bulb in case she made an appearance again. Sure enough, as I looked out a downstairs window, I saw her arrive in a horse-drawn coach." Royston's speech quickened. "This time I grabbed my camera and rushed out, only to find the coach gone. I spotted her, however, heading toward the orchard again, and I called for her to stop. I was a good distance from her, about twenty feet or so, and I had my camera in hand. Raising it carefully, I stopped, braced myself and took a shot." Royston ceased talking and fell back into his chair.

Robertson scribbled more notes before speaking. "Have you developed that photo, Mr. Royston? Did you get her picture?" His voice rose, and he spoke in what was practically a screech.

Royston grabbed the folder at his feet. Smiling, he selected one and offered it to the young reporter. Robertson's eyes bulged like a boy seeing a magician's trick. The photograph showed what appeared to be an apparition of a woman, like what Royston had described. From the back, she seemed to float above the ground and was entering the orchard, with trees all around her. A halo of light surrounded her gowned figure.

Robertson spoke without taking his eyes from the image. "This is astounding, Mr. Royston. I believe you have captured the image of a ghost. That is, of course, impossible, but here it is in my hands. May I take this with me to show my editor?"

"Of course, David, you certainly may. Take the entire folder. The other photos are of rooms in the house, with my mother posed in them. I simply offer them as additional points of interest. I have the negatives and can reproduce the images whenever I wish. Your editor will find that folder quite interesting."

"Indeed he will, Mr. Royston. Thank you very much."

The article ran in the Nashua newspaper and caused quite a stir. Though many scoffed at the picture of the ghostly image as a camera trick, nobody could stop those wanting to believe in ghosts from doing just that. The article was a big success for Allan Royston, and the number of believers increased steadily, especially during the times surrounding the full moon. He began selling tours of the house and property.

Allan Royston and his mother churned a small living from the tours and items for sale in the house. The most popular item was the picture of the beautiful, ghostly image of a tall woman fleeing into the orchard. Allan touched them up to add reddish hair to the figure. He captioned the picture "The Ghost of Ocean Born Mary."

Chapter Thirteen
Saturday, September 6, 1975, Henniker, New Hampshire

    I decided to let Bart conduct his early morning training session unencumbered by a visit from his sister. I had Sam next to me in bed, and I wasn't in a hurry to get up. He was still sleeping, flat on his back, and I relished the sight of him. Another moment of staring was all I could take.
    My hand slipped under the covers, caressing his bare chest, and his face broke into a smile as his eyes opened. I took that as my cue to snuggle close to his side, my fingers moving across his skin. "Good morning, lover boy," I whispered. "Got any plans for today?"
    "I can't think beyond this delightful moment, dear girl. Just want to keep the blood flowing."
    My hand moved lower on him, and I found what I was looking for. "Your blood is flowing perfectly well, Mr. Sam." I kissed him, caressed him and joined with him. Our passion grew and grew, our bodies undulating, pounding together, and finally we meshed in a powerful climax. Afterward we drifted off to more sleep.

    The pleasing aroma of bacon sizzling floated upstairs to my room, and I awoke alone. I slipped into a New Sussex College soccer shirt that I had owned for years and sometimes used as a nightgown. It was still resting at the foot of my bed from the night before.
    Sam was fully dressed in jeans and a red shirt. His sleeves were rolled up to the elbow, and it was unbuttoned at the collar. He smelled of the Old Spice soap he showered

with, and his hair was neatly combed. His aroma was better to me than the bacon.

I gave him a quick hug from behind, sliding my arms around his waist. After a gentle pat on his rear, I found a coffee mug and filled it from the pot beside the stove. Sam turned to me as I slid onto a chair at the table. "Great timing, Martha. The scrambles will be ready in a jiff."

I loved it when Sam served me breakfast. It was a treat usually reserved for weekends that never grew old.

"What time are you going over to the house?" asked Sam. We had started referring Bart's new property as *the house*. Saying the Ocean Born Mary house was an oral burden.

"Let's wait until this afternoon. I want to give Teresa some time to get comfortable before we show up like a couple of inspectors. Do you think Auggie will pull any crap today?"

Sam chomped on a slice of bacon. "He wasn't real thrilled about Bart hiring Teresa, that's for sure. But I don't know what sort of research he can do on a Saturday, other than checking at the Historical Society. Maybe he's going to hold Monty Phillips to that promise to offer consultation."

"He didn't exactly make a promise, Sam. I kind of trapped his pompous ass into that one. But I think you're right. There isn't much else Auggie can do today. The Historical Society has morning hours on Saturdays, and I'll bet Auggie will start there. I'm sure Monty will want to check out Teresa after he hears about her. It could make for an interesting afternoon."

I passed the morning hours by doing some grocery shopping at the Henniker Market, and Sam caught up on his laundry at my place. He didn't have a washer and dryer at his apartment, and it was cheaper to use mine than visit the laundromat. *We sure are getting domestic.*

We made our way to the house by two o'clock and were pleased to see several cars parked along the road. People were arriving as others left. It looked like a good day for the haunted house business.

The young woman who had served Sam stew was dressed in colonial clothing and greeted us at the door, tickets in hand, looking ready to take our money. Sam entered first, and she smiled at him in an inviting way, but turned a frown as I passed by. The feeling was mutual.

"We're just looking for Bart. You know, *my brother,*" I said.

"Well, he's on a tour right now, probably in the backyard. You're welcome to wait inside," she replied, again with the smile at Sam, who took too long smiling back. My hand found his butt and pushed him forward.

We heard voices from the parlor and turned toward them. Lucy and Teresa were inside guiding customers through the room full of trinkets, photos and other junk. Teresa's hair was loose at shoulder length, but she wore contemporary clothing—a blue jumper over a white blouse. Lucy was in full colonial garb.

"Sam, take a look at that." I poked him in the ribs and pointed to a large photo print on the wall above the mantel. It was a black and white photograph with a ghostly-looking image of a woman, shown from behind. She seemed to be floating into an orchard. A light surrounded her entire body and, although the picture was black and white, her hair was tinted light red.

"That's a very nice print," said Sam, his eyes fixed on it. "It really seems spooky. Even seems old, judging by the brown tint around the edges."

"It is old," croaked Lucy from a few feet away. "And authentic. Well, sort of. That image was taken by Allan Royston when he owned the place, and it ran in a Nashua newspaper in 1931. The print on the wall is a photocopy that Bart made from the original."

"Where'd he get that?" I asked.

"From me." A voice sounded from behind us, and I turned to find Monty Phillips walking toward us, with Auggie right behind. Monty reached back to place a hand on Auggie's shoulder. "Mr. Raymond was searching in the Historical Society awhile back and liked the picture he found in our collection. I never thought much of it, since it's a fraud, of course. I must admit, however, that it's a well-manipulated rendition."

Auggie waved downward, urging Monty to keep his voice down.

"Oh, don't worry, Auggie. Photographers have been retouching pictures for as long as the first tintype. As I said; it's very well done, and I believe it is quite effective. Now, let's have a look at that woman you told me about." Monty looked about the room and quickly found Teresa. "Ah-hah. That must be her. Please introduce us."

I glimpsed a smile from Teresa as the men approached her. Only Monty returned the cordial look. Auggie frowned at his mother, who nodded. As Auggie made the introductions, Monty sized her up. His eyes went from face to foot and back up again, his hand grazing her red hair. Teresa didn't react to the inspection, as if expecting it. Monty's face gave him away. He was hooked.

I leaned in toward Sam and whispered, "You were right about where Auggie would start his verification process."

Another voice surprised us. "The next tour begins in five minutes, folks. We'll start in the dining room, so please gather there." It was Bart. "You've got that one, Auggie."

His partner looked relieved and slid away after sending a glance to Monty, as if it were a message. Monty nodded at him in return.

"Good afternoon, Mr. Sanborn," said Monty, extending his hand to Bart for a quick greeting. Bart shook the hand.

"I'm impressed with your new employee, Bart. Auggie told me all about your meeting with her yesterday. I must say, she is very beautiful, especially those green eyes and long, red hair. The hair can be colored artificially, but those eyes are certainly genuine. Dressed appropriately, she would truly resemble the description of Mary Wallace of Londonderry." He spoke as if Teresa wasn't really there.

"Don't get ahead of yourself, Phillips," said Bart. "Nobody said anything about playing dress up. Teresa is on a two-week trial as a worker here. We haven't made any plans beyond that. I'm sure Auggie has told you about our talk yesterday."

"Yes, of course. I'll check into the matter soon, but I wanted to get a firsthand look. I admit to being impressed. She is remarkable, but I'd like to make some calls to a few colleagues before making any statement." Monty seemed snobbier with every word.

I admired Teresa's poise through this whole discussion. She didn't utter a sound.

The stuffed shirt gave a polite nod and made his exit. I gave a look to Sam that said, *I thought he'd never leave.*

Sam and I decided to leave as well, and I said goodbye to Bart and the ladies.

"Wait, I'll walk you out," said Bart. We stepped past Bart's friend at the front door and into the front yard, where we could see Monty driving away. "Thanks for coming by, Martha. What do you think about Monty's reaction? I guess he wasn't convinced."

"Don't read too much into that guy's talk. That part about making a few calls was just to impress us. It was just a way of declaring his self-importance," I said.

"Perhaps you're right. I'd sure like to see people's reactions if Teresa were dressed for the part. Would folks notice her likeness to the photograph? Maybe I need some frontal images of Mary Wallace. Too bad there aren't any."

"Maybe you should make some," chimed Sam.

It was Labor Day, and a welcomed day off. Sam was out for a while, giving me some space and getting some of his own. The phone rang, and it took three rings before I could slug my way to it. When I did, the unhappy voice on the other end was Bart's, fussing about wanting to see me right away at my apartment. I didn't like the sound of it. *What now?*

When he arrived, I steered him to the kitchen and took a seat at the table, expecting him to follow suit. But he was too agitated, so he paced the floor instead. He didn't need coffee, so I poured two bourbons, slipping one into his hand before I took a load off my feet.

"Okay, Bart, what gives?"

He swallowed some Jim Beam before answering. "I got a call an hour ago from Teresa. She told me about a meeting she'd had earlier today at the Historical Society with Monty and Auggie. I wasn't invited."

"What? Go on."

"She said it was too bad I couldn't make it, but I had already seen her documents, so it probably didn't matter. She said it went well, and Monty was quite impressed with the story of her lineage to the Wallace family. They were so pleased at the end that Auggie and Monty even hugged. She said Monty is completely on board now. It was all I could do to keep my cool. Can you believe this? Auggie and Monty set up this meeting and didn't tell me a word about it. That had to be intentional. You don't just accidentally have a business meeting without your partner."

"Bart, we know that Auggie met with Monty Phillips on Saturday to try and verify Teresa's story. Monty came back to the house with Auggie so he could see her for himself. At what point did they decide to set a meeting for today?"

My brother grew more agitated and knocked down more Beam. "I don't know. That's the problem. They intentionally left me out. I can't believe it." He was getting red faced.

I tried to find a legitimate reason why Bart wasn't told about the meeting, to calm the guy down if nothing else. "I'm sure Monty wanted to see those documents. The, ah, receipts from the school. You had already seen them, as Teresa pointed out, so maybe Auggie didn't think it was necessary to have you there. That's reasonable to me. I don't think there's an evil conspiracy going on. Did you ask Auggie about it?"

Bart shook his head, cradling his bourbon with both hands. "No, I called you right away and left the house immediately. I wanted to let off some steam before confronting him."

"That was the best decision you've made today. I hope it works and you calm down before you see him, which you will have to do sometime today. Look, you two are partners and old friends. There has to be trust between you, or your enterprise is going up in smoke. Don't forget: when it comes to the money, you did the heavy lifting, so you have to make this work." I waited for his response.

Bart eased more Beam down his throat, set his glass down and stood up, pushing his chair away from the table. "You may be right, Mart, but I'm still pissed off that they did this. I'm going to go talk to him about it right now."

Bart had calmed down a little, but I felt he was still on the borderline. A confrontation with Auggie could go either way. I decided he needed another person on his side, since he'd be outnumbered by Auggie and his dear old mom. "I'll follow you over, Bart. I don't want things to get out of hand."

My brother gave me a tight smile. "I don't suppose I can talk you out of it All right, come along." Bart headed for the front door.

"Just let me leave a note for Sam." I found an old envelope and pen nearby, scribbled the quick message, "At the House," and left it on the table. I was a car length behind Bart the whole way back.

After parking, I had to run to catch up with Bart, entering the house a few seconds after him. I was just in time to see him hustle into the parlor, where Lucy was dusting off the merchandise on the tables. His voice was calm, but it had an edge to it. "Where's Auggie? I need to talk to him."

The old lady pointed to the ceiling. She wasn't much for conversation.

Bart darted into the hallway and called from the bottom stair. "Auggie, come on down, please. We need to talk."

At least he is calm enough to say please. That's a good sign. The problem with good signs is that sometimes they don't mean anything.

Before Auggie could make it halfway down, Bart was on him. "What the hell is the fucking idea of meeting without me today? What the hell are you up to?"

Auggie held both palms facing Bart as he continued his descent. "Whoa, big fellow. Hold on. Don't get all lathered up. You want to talk? Okay, let's talk, but we don't have to shout. Come on." He motioned us into the dining room, where we claimed seats around the big, circular table; Lucy, Auggie, Bart and me.

I was eager to see how Auggie would handle this.

"Are you talking about my session this morning with Monty and Teresa?"

"Of course that's what I'm talking about," snapped Bart.

"I'm glad Monty brought you up to speed on it. He's really interested in the business now. The meeting went very well."

Bart's voice grew louder, and the veins in his neck were bulging. "It wasn't Monty Phillips who told me. It was Teresa. She had the decency to call me, a lot more than my *partner* did. Where do you think you get off shutting me out like that?"

"Easy boy, easy does it. Nobody shut you out. Look, Monty was very impressed with Teresa after he met her, and I saw him downtown on Sunday. It was just a chance thing. He said he'd like to have the meeting with me and

Teresa, so he could see her documents and hear her tell the story of her lineage."

Before Bart could say anything, I reacted. "See, Bart, I told you it was probably like that. There's no cause for alarm." Bart didn't seem to hear me.

"I understand you and Monty got quite buddy-buddy. How'd you manage to swing that? That's not how you two looked on Saturday."

Auggie folded his hands on the table. "Look Bart, Monty turns out to be a very reasonable guy if you give him a chance. He looked over the documents very carefully, believe me, and he listened to every word Teresa had to say. He even drew out a sketch of her family tree as she explained it. He doesn't think anybody could have made that up on the spot, so he said he believes her—although he told me after Teresa left that he'll still check the names out in Londonderry, just to be sure."

Bart got angrier, despite the explanation, and he rose from his chair. "So you and Monty had a pow-wow even after dismissing Teresa? What else did you talk about?"

"Really Bart, that's none of your concern. We had finished the business meeting, Teresa went on her way and we just kept chatting about things in general, that's all."

"Just chatting, eh? Things in general, eh? Well I hope that's all it was, because if you two are cooking anything up behind my back, you'll be sorry." Bart slammed his hand on the table. "There might be a new ghost in this house."

Bart pushed his way past me and ran outside. I hadn't seen my brother lose his temper like that since we were kids.

Auggie unfolded his hands, arms stretched out on the table, and gave me a smirk. "I think that went well, Martha."

Very funny.

I ran out after Bart and caught up with him near his car.

"Bart, wait."

He stopped and turned toward me, and I saw that look in his eyes. Sometimes, when we were kids, Bart would get into a squabble with a family member or a friend, and he'd be all hell fire. But after a cooling off, his face showed a sadness that came out of the blue, as if he'd just watched himself acting like a complete ass and knew it.

"Mart, I'm sorry that I got so heated up, but sometimes Auggie can do that to me. You know how it is."

"Yes, I'm afraid I do."

Bart looked at his feet while I squeezed his arm, but in a moment, he lifted his head and spoke as if he had just gotten a great idea. "There's one person who can straighten this all out."

Uh-oh. Who might that be? There weren't too many players in this scene, so he had me concerned. He read my look easily.

"Now, don't get excited, Mart. I'm going to call on Teresa. She told me she took an apartment above Henniker Market, and I owe her a thank you for the call today. It won't take long."

I felt a lump in my throat. Bart's emotions could turn on a dime, and it seemed to be happening again. I didn't like this idea, but tried to be reassuring.

"Well, okay. Maybe that's the right thing to do. I'll come along."

"There's no need to do that. I'm calm now, really I am, and I wasn't mad at Teresa, anyway. I'll be fine."

"I'm sure you will be, but I need to get to know her better, and this is a good chance to do that. I don't want to cramp your style, so I won't stay long. I'll follow in my car. Let's go." I didn't give Bart a chance to argue and headed for my vehicle.

Parking was nose first in front of the market, and two open spaces were separated by an old pick-up truck. A wooden staircase on the side of the building led up to an entrance that opened into a straight hall running along the front of the second story. Three apartments divided the structure, with doors numbered for each one. Bart led me to number three.

After two knocks, a voice called out softly. "Who is it?"

"Hi, Teresa, it's Bart Sanborn. Got a minute?"

"For you, of course, Bart." The door swung open, and Teresa's face went from a smile to disappointment when she saw me.

I had to look up at her. "Hi, I'm Bart's sister, Martha. Remember me?"

"Of course I do, silly. It was just the other day when we met. Please, come in."

We stepped into a neatly made up little apartment: a kitchenette, small table and a sitting area with a sofa, chair and a TV on a bookshelf. A door at the back suggested a bedroom and bath. She offered soft drinks, and we accepted.

"Please, sit while I get the beverages," she said. I took the only chair, and Bart settled on the end of the sofa. I watched Bart's face as Teresa moved gently about the room, reaching for glasses from a cabinet and then taking ice from the fridge. She moved with grace. Bart looked hypnotized by her movements. She had on tight jeans, a T-shirt and bare feet, but you'd think she was in an elegant evening gown the way Bart looked at her.

"Thank you again, Teresa, for calling me today. I'm glad the meeting you had was productive." It seemed strange. When Bart talked to me about the meeting, he was filled with rage. Talking to Teresa about the same event, he was all quiet and cordial.

She served us, and I put my glass on an end table within reach of both me and Bart. He did the same after taking a swallow. Teresa eased onto the middle of the sofa, close to Bart. She sat back on her seat, but kept straight, not quite touching the backrest. Her legs were crossed and her hands folded on the top one. She could have been a model.

"I understand Monty is going to be a supporter of the project. You and Auggie must have used magic to swing the guy. He seemed so suspicious and doubtful at first." Bart was starting his dig for information.

"He was a little stiff at first, but he was fascinated with the receipts I had, and he said he believed what I told them about being related to Mary Wallace. He says resemblance to the physical description of Ocean Born Mary is something we need to exploit to the fullest. He promised to work with Auggie on finding the best way to do that."

Bart gave me a look. I think he was about to take off on those two again, but Teresa's voice stopped him.

"You know, my childhood was rather lonely, and we never had any of the wealth of the Wallace family. But I'm glad my family never tried to take their money. I can't complain. A good family is better than money alone."

Oh my, there she goes. When she'd spoken like that before, I felt for her. Of course, she was in the same room as Auggie and Monty, so she sounded good. But this time I felt she was pouring it on a bit.

There it was. Like the strike of a cobra, her hands unfolded and one reached for Bart, touching his thigh. Just as fast, they were back in the folded position on her own leg. "I feel like I'm part of a family again."

Bart flashed a smile at her.

He's feeling better, too, I'm sure. Bart gazed at her with sympathetic eyes. His pulse must be quickening.

If she was putting on maneuvers, she was very effective. This man, who moments before, was ready to tear out the jugular vein of his partner, was becoming as subdued as a pussycat.

There it is again, the cobra strike, hand to thigh. "I'll be right back, so don't go away," she said before gliding into her kitchenette again. There was just enough twitch to her tush to make Bart's eyes almost burst from his head. I'd have been disgusted with the maneuver if I hadn't used it myself on occasion. When I did it to Sam, I could almost feel his eyes on me.

Teresa rattled some crackers out of a box and onto a tray and brought them back with her. She resumed her position, legs crossed, hands folded, but this time she was a tad closer to Bart. *Oh, brother.*

"I think Monty is absolutely right, Teresa, you *are* the image of Ocean Born Mary. That's the way we'll go about it. We don't even have to fake it. You are related to her, so a resemblance is perfectly believable."

"Too bad there aren't any old paintings of Mary that show her face." I groaned.

"We can take care of that," said Bart. "Sam said it himself—maybe we can make some. I know somebody in Manchester who's pretty good with a brush. Teresa can sit for her, and we'll post the finished product in the house."

"But Bart, dear, surely people won't believe that they are originals." Teresa smiled at Bart, her eyes penetrating his.

"We won't try to fool anybody. I'll caption the image as a likeness only. If pressed on the matter, we'll gladly admit that Teresa sat for an artist. The point is to have a visual of Ocean Born Mary that people will associate with Teresa, one that shows her face. We also have the one that Allan Royston made of a ghostly woman walking into the orchard. We'll let the public's imagination take care of the rest. I tell you, people want to believe this legend so badly that it hurts them. It's going to be great. We might have to give you a raise, Teresa."

"Easy, Bart," I said. "She still has a two-week trial period, remember? Let's be calm and get through that first."

"She already has, as far as I'm concerned," he replied. "It sounds as if Auggie and Monty are convinced, too." He leaned toward Teresa. "I'm going to make a call right now and set up the sitting for my artist friend. The sooner, the better. Don't you agree?"

This time both of her hands found Bart's leg. "Oh, Bart, that would be great. I'll be happy to pose for her."

I took her two-handed touch as a signal for me to make my exit. Rising from my chair, I said it was time to go check up on Sam.

"Are you leaving, too, Bart?" Teresa made it sound like an invitation.

"Ah, no, if you don't mind me using your phone."

Bart's pants showed slight dents under Teresa's fingers. She was squeezing his leg.

"Don't get up, kiddies, I can find my way out."

The couple said goodbye to me, and I was out the door and descending the long, outside steps. *Boy, this girl is good.*

Is she really interested in Bart or is this all a ploy, as Monty first suspected? Maybe she is on her way to joining the family, or maybe she is trying to con a con-man.

Chapter Fourteen
Saturday, September 13, 1975, Henniker, New Hampshire

Bart was right about Auggie and Monty approving Teresa before her trial period was up. It was like their skepticism had never existed, as if she held some magical powers over them all.

Sam and I started our weekend in the usual fashion, beginning at home before making our way to the house in the late morning. The place was buzzing with patrons. It was move-in day at the college, so I guess we were getting some residual traffic from the incoming parents who wanted to check out this legend. I found out why later. Auggie had placed copies of his pamphlet in the lobbies of all the dorms. He was planning on giving a talk at the house and had done what he could to help boost the attendance.

We had agreed to help with food from the kitchen. Our task was to make sandwiches and various snacks. I unpacked loaves of bread that we brought from the market, while Sam perused the kitchen for utensils. "Hey Martha, look at this." Sam stood at a counter near the stove. There was a block with old looking knives, long handled forks and spoons.

He had drawn a vintage kitchen knife out of the block. It looked old enough to have belonged to the original owners of the house. Sam clutched the handle and swished it through the air like a pirate's sword.

"Better be careful with that thing, buster, before you decapitate somebody. You're having too much fun."

His face showed the disappointment of a kid whose mother had just rained on his parade.

"This is a beauty, Martha. How old do you think it is?" Sam held the knife with both hands, extending the big blade toward me. I made out the initials *DM* and the number 3 raised on the blade.

"I can't tell, Sam, but it looks as though it might have been made by hand." I ran my finger along the finely crafted steel.

Sam stood beside me at the big table and started slicing the loaves with his newfound toy. "It's got a good edge, slices well. This could take a finger off a careless colonial."

We made sandwiches of sliced meats with lettuce and tomato, but held back on the condiments. A collection of small, plastic packages of mayo, ketchup and mustard were available. The sandwiches, on plastic plates and covered with clear wrap, were spread out on the kitchen table for sale. The extras were put in a tall fridge in the back mudroom that served as storage. A soda machine had been installed beside it.

The two o'clock tour was about to start. I could hear Auggie giving introductory remarks in the parlor before herding the people into the dining room. He sounded like a sideshow pitchman. PT Barnum could have used this guy.

Bart showed himself, said a quick hello, and said he was going to help at the front door until it was time for his turn at conducting a tour. He seemed to sour when I mentioned Auggie's excitement, but showed a light in his eye when Teresa's name came up. "You'll enjoy her part in today's work, just wait."

My brother was falling hard.

Auggie pointed out that the group would return to the parlor for a special surprise at the end of the tour. But first, he had a story to tell. "As we move out of this splendid parlor, take a look at this fine painting on the wall. We've just received it from an artist who was commissioned by our company to render a likeness of a young Mary Wallace, the one and only Ocean Born Mary. Using as much descriptive information as we could supply from our records—as well as those from the Henniker Historical Society—and a current model, the artist completed this beautiful work yesterday. As you can see, Mary must have been a tall, trim young beauty with flowing reddish hair, long arms and slender hands. Whether one believes in ghosts or not, Mary is truly still here because of that painting."

The group of eight filed past the wall displaying the art work, and Auggie kept them moving at a slow pace to allow them to see the image of Mary. They gathered in the dining room, crowding around the table.

"Feel free to take a seat, if you wish," offered the tour guide. After some shuffled into seats, Auggie got his act going. "I'll start by telling you about the astonishing history of Ocean Born Mary and this grand house."

I peered through the doorway from the kitchen to see Auggie in action. The group was enthralled by the story of a pirate attack on the vessel containing Scots-Irish immigrants, including James and the pregnant Elizabeth Wilson. Some sat with mouths open, and one woman shed a tear when he related the tale of the pirate sparing the immigrants once he saw baby Mary, whose green eyes reminded him of his lost love.

When Auggie talked about the elderly Mary Wallace moving to Henniker, he gave a version of the story that differed considerably from the facts as I had learned them over my years living in Henniker. I listened with great interest.

The Auggie version got creative. He told about the pirate, whom he claimed was named Don Pedro, coming to the Wallace house after a long search for Ocean Born Mary. According to Auggie, the pirate was some twenty years her elder and was compelled to find the girl with the emerald eyes. Having traced her to New Hampshire, he soon learned of her whereabouts and showed up unannounced in Henniker. He was charming and won the heart of the widowed Mary Wallace, eventually getting her to marry him. With the great wealth he had acquired as a pirate, Don Pedro built this great house for his bride.

It didn't take long for me to figure out what Auggie was up to. The arrival of Don Pedro into Mary's life, true or not, was essential to his plan. He went on to twist the story into a tale of lost treasure. With Don Pedro being a resident of the Wallace house, Auggie was able to embellish the yarn, adding inferences that treasure lay hidden somewhere on the grounds. Now the tale contained not only something for ghost lovers, but for fans of pirate stories and hidden treasure.

Auggie had lots more gall than brains. I couldn't believe his next move, which involved pulling a document from his pocket and reading a passage he claimed was written by Mary. It suggested that Don Pedro had built a thriving apple orchard, and it was, "not the only source of wealth to be found on the grounds." I couldn't help blurting out a laugh, and I quickly struggled to stifle it, disguising it as a cough. Auggie shot an eye dart at me as I retreated into the kitchen to tell Sam.

"What's so funny, Miss? Or are you coming down with something?" At least Sam found me amusing.

"Sam, Auggie's out there dishing some cock and bull story about pirate treasure on the property. I bet he's setting up another way to separate tourists from their money. He even produced a document as some sort of proof, but I'm sure it's fake."

Sam didn't seem fazed by Auggie's move. "Hey, you've got to hand it to him. The guy has some slick moves. The idea is to make money, so let's see how he plans to add this idea to his cash flow gimmicks."

Sam and I went back to our places, ready to offer sandwiches to the group as they passed through the kitchen and out into the backyard. We sold several. Auggie declined to take one, offering me a glare instead. There were many visitors who were not part of the tour, and we sold some food to them. Others could be heard talking to Lucy and her helpers in the parlor.

When the tour was reaching its conclusion, I heard Auggie instructing them to reenter the kitchen and collect in the parlor. They did so, buzzing about the house and the possibility of treasure on the ground. A few seemed to dismiss the idea, but many voiced interest to each other in hushed tones. Their voices grew loud enough for me to hear as they marched by.

Once he had them properly corralled, Auggie stood near the door between the parlor and the front hall. "Ladies and gentlemen, I promised you a surprise before you left today, and now is the time to reveal it." He angled his head toward the tall stairway and called, "Teresa, would you please join us?"

Sam and I were under the archway connecting the kitchen and the dining room, so we couldn't see her. I motioned Sam forward, and we maneuvered out to the rear of the hall for a better view. The tall, beautiful Teresa had descended the stairs and then strode through the hall into the parlor, where she stood next to Auggie. She wore an elegant gown that looked like it belonged in the eighteenth century, and her reddish hair hung loosely around her face, reaching below her shoulders in length. I looked at the faces in the crowd and saw many smiles, along with some blank stares.

"Folks, I'd like you to meet Teresa Thurgood, a direct descendant of Mary Wallace, also known as Ocean Born Mary." There was a momentary silence, followed by polite applause. As the clapping slowed, a man standing near the new portrait of Mary spoke out. "Hey, she looks like the woman in this painting. That's convenient. I thought you said an artist made it up from records."

"I did," said Auggie. "But I also said he had a current model. You see, we were very fortunate to have Teresa come into our lives recently. Let me tell you about that."

Auggie went on to tell the tale of her arrival in Henniker, and the story of her lineage. As he was speaking, Monty Phillips made a timely entrance from the back, nodding to me as he worked his way up to Auggie and Teresa.

"Folks, my name is Monty Phillips. I'm a professor of History at New Sussex College and Director of the Henniker Historical Society, a place I hope you will visit sometime. I have interviewed Ms. Thurgood at length and have researched her claim to being a descendant of Ocean Born Mary. From the records I have seen, including what she showed from her own documents, I have concluded that her claim is authentic. Oh, and don't forget the physical resemblance, especially those lovely green eyes."

People near her reached out to shake her hand. Others looked her up and down, as if examining an artifact, and people in the back of the room stood on tiptoes or stretched their necks to get a better view. After a short while, a gentle applause echoed in the room.

People began to ask Teresa questions, even after Auggie officially concluded the tour. "People, Teresa is going to be working in the parlor, where we have many interesting souvenirs for sale, and she'll do her best to answer your questions."

Teresa eased her way past the tourists, light on her feet as always. Folks willingly stepped aside, creating a path for her that sealed up quickly after she went by. She took up a place at a table next to a grim-faced Lucy. She tried to push the souvenirs, but people were more interested in her red hair, her smooth skin, her elegant gown and—most of all—her emerald eyes. She relished the attention and turned it to an advantage.

Teresa manipulated the conversations masterfully, combining answers to questions with sales pitches for a trinket or two. Before they knew it, each tourist was caught in a small purchase. Sale after sale added up to a respectable addition to the cash flow for the day.

The tours held nearly the same number of people all day, a pleasant state of affairs for Bart and Auggie. Teresa was pleased too, quite satisfied that she had proven her value. Her first day's success was not going to be lost on her bosses if she had anything to say about it, and she did.

After the visitors and lady helpers were gone, Sam and I remained with Teresa. The partners—along with Teresa, Sam and I—decided to have coffee at the dining room table. It was time for Teresa to put her thoughts out there for Auggie and Bart.

"This was a wonderful day," she offered in her come-hither voice. "I loved the way the tourists responded to me. They couldn't stop talking to me. I had to cut some of them off in order to allow somebody else to step forward at the table. I hated doing that, but well, what else could I do? And they just kept buying things." She gave a girlish squeal.

Bart's eyes seemed to be staring through her face. "They couldn't get enough of you, Teresa. You were wonderful. You're a natural for the work."

She didn't let that remark slip by. "Bart, I think you're right. I even surprised myself, feeling so comfortable with the people. Maybe I could even conduct a tour myself sometime. It would be like Mary was taking them around her house. If all the tourists are as responsive as today, I think they'd love it."

Bart's face lit up and his eyes widened. She was reeling him in.

"Hold on a minute," groused Auggie. "Let's not get ahead of ourselves. Yes, Teresa did a wonderful job today, but it is very early." He looked at Teresa and softened his voice. "You did great, no doubt, but you need more experience before you can do a tour. I think we'll get to that someday, but let's not rush. Besides, you pulled in a lot of sales working the parlor today, and we don't want to lose that."

"Oh, Auggie, come off it," said Bart. "She'll make even more money for us as a tour guide. Once we get some publicity out there about her, our attendance will jump. More tourists mean more sales. You'll see."

Auggie bit his lip, like he wanted to explode, but held back. Lucy watched her son.

Before the discussion could go any further, Teresa stood up and excused herself. "I'm beat, so I'll be getting along now. Goodnight, everybody." I guess Teresa felt she had accomplished all she could today. She had become the center of attention for the tourists and had planted a seed in Bart's mind about her greater value. *Smart move.*

Bart stood as she left the table, looking unhappy that Teresa had made her exit. Auggie seemed relieved. Both remained silent. I made the mistake of opening my mouth.

"You have to admit that Ms. Thurgood was a big hit today, and she didn't need any help from some pirate drivel."

"What the hell is that supposed to mean?" barked Auggie. "The pirate story will lure people here. It has nothing to do with Teresa. Don't you get it, Ms. Sanborn?"

"I get it, all right. I get that pulling out that crummy paper and implying that it's some kind of proof that pirate treasure exists on the grounds is the kind of phony move that will get you nowhere."

"You know, Ms. Sanborn, I'm getting rather sick of your remarks and giggles, especially when I'm working the crowd. Why don't you get your ass out of here before somebody spanks it?"

Sam leaned forward. "Be careful with your mouth, Auggie, or you might lose a few teeth."

Bart jumped in, glaring at his partner. "Don't even think about it, Auggie. You'll have more trouble than you can handle. If you so much as put a hand on my sister, I'll beat your head in, get it?"

"All right, everybody, just calm down." I didn't want this to get out of hand. "What the hell are you all getting steamed up for? You had a very successful day today, but you'd never know it. There's no need to be bashing each other or making threats. Teresa did exactly what you hoped she'd do. She won over the tourists, and money went into the cash box as a result. Okay, so Teresa needs more time before she takes on a tour. There's no need to rush."

"What the hell? You're taking his side?" Bart's neck veins were showing.

"It's not a matter of taking sides." I lowered my voice. "I have no vested interest in this business. I'm giving you my objective opinion, that's all. Teresa's going to be a money maker for you, but I think you should keep things going like today for a bit longer. Let the word get out about her. Like you said, Bart, get some publicity going. Hey, Halloween is not far off. Be thinking about how you'll handle that night."

I felt guilty about laughing during Auggie's presentation and apologized. "I'm sorry, Auggie. I promise not to giggle again." He gave me a snort that I took as an acceptance. *If he ever tries to spank me, I'll kick his ass.*

Bart said nothing. He hustled his way out of the dining room and left the house. I think I knew where he was going.

Chapter Fifteen
Sunday, September 14, 1975, Henniker, New Hampshire

Summer's end. Leaves turning colors and falling, brightening the New Hampshire landscape. A magnificent ritual of nature, something one could count on year after year. The beauty of the rolling hills gleaming with magnificent colors spawned a tourist industry all its own. On weekends, the highways filled with cars from southern New England, bringing people into this realm of color. The season was another source of potential customers for the Ocean Born Mary house. As long as they were in the area, well-crafted publicity could draw many of them in.

We had promised to help out with leaf raking at the house, so Sam and I spent over an hour laboring to clear the yard. I hadn't raked leaves for many years, since I didn't have my own property. I wore faded jeans and a three-quarter sleeve athletic shirt Sam had given me, along with hiking boots. My arms grew weary from working the wide fan rake, but we had fun building the leaf piles on top of an old blanket and hauling the catch off to a spot into the trees, clearing an area close to the house.

When a pile got sufficiently large, Sam couldn't resist the urge for boyish play. He'd catch me by surprise from behind. Cradling me in his arms face down, he rolled me into the stack of color. Then he'd start covering me with leaves before I could get up. It took my mind off the display of temper shown by Bart and Auggie the day before.

We did our fair share of yard work for the morning, clearing the front yard completely from the road up to the house. I was tired and hungry by eleven-thirty. Sam concurred with my suggestion to go back to my place to clean up and have lunch.

"I'm a mess," I said as I exited Sam's car back home. "Time for a shower."

"Need some help with that?" Always the gentleman.

We lathered each other in the shower, rinsed and embraced before this wonderful moment between us ended. Showering with Sam had become a special escape for me, ever since the time the previous year when we'd had a close call with a motorist trying to send us into the Contoocook River. Being in his arms while the warm shower water caressed us gave me a moment to appreciate how important he had become to me. I closed my eyes and buried my head against his chest.

After drying, we dressed for the second time that day. It was warm enough for some tight cut off shorts, white Levi's being my choice. I slid into a dark blue T-shirt and old tennis shoes to complete my ensemble. Sam chose Levi's, too, but went with long ones, and he donned a white V-neck. Sam wasn't big on formal exercise, but he didn't have to be. He was still trim and strong looking, with lean muscle in his arms and a flat stomach.

I led our two-person parade into the kitchen, where I suggested tuna fish sandwiches. Sam poured the soda, while I mixed the tuna. We sat at the kitchen table, assembling our sandwiches with lettuce, sliced onion and tomato. I stared into Sam's eyes and decided that this was a good time to talk about something that was on my mind.

"Sam, you know I have my doubts about Auggie. I know they had a successful day yesterday, and their little enterprise seems to be off to a good start, but I'm still worried."

Sam put his sandwich up to his mouth as I spoke but held off from taking a bite. "You know Auggie a lot better than I do, but from what I've seen so far, he just looks like a slick hustler. Do you think it goes deeper than that?"

"I'm sure of it. I figure Bart has also gotten into things he won't tell me about. But what bothers me right now is their relationship. Bart seems to be very distrustful of Auggie, and I think the feeling is mutual. With Lucy in the picture, Bart is outnumbered. It's getting to be a bad situation. It's not like Bart to be making physical threats, Sam. I'm worried."

Sam swallowed a bite of tuna and washed it down with a swig of soda. "If you mean that little blow up yesterday after Auggie suggested you needed a spanking, that was just a big brother looking after his little sister. I wouldn't fret about it."

"But there was also Bart's getting riled up about the secret meeting with Teresa and Monty. Those two seem to be getting further apart as the business gets more successful. And Auggie and Monty are rather strange bedfellows, if you ask me. They seem to have gotten rather buddy-buddy lately. If it weren't for Teresa, I'd be afraid that Bart could be getting nosed out."

Sam smiled at me and reached across the table to touch my hand. "Don't forget, he's the majority owner. He's got a solid position, Martha."

"Maybe you're right, but I still don't like the looks of things between him and Auggie. Sam, I want you to help me with this. Will you?"

Sam nodded, swallowed more sandwich and smiled. "Of course I'll help you, but I don't see anything for us to do right now."

I took a deep breath. "Look, you got to know Chief Cal Powers pretty well last year. Maybe you could go talk to him and just ask if he could check on Auggie, that's all. I'd like to know if there is something specific in his past that we should know about. I'm sure Cal would be willing to do a favor like that. After all, you did solve a murder for him and uncover a corrupt young cop in his department. What do you say?"

"You're forgetting that he wasn't real happy about the way Eli and I were going to handle that situation with an ex-Nazi. But you're right. We did save his bacon. Okay, I'll stop by his office and chat with him sometime tomorrow. Feel better?"

"Yes, Sam, I do." *Bad choice of words. I didn't want to sound like a bride.* "Oops, sorry, no pun intended, Sammy."

He looked flushed for a second. We were two divorcees trying to keep our relationship well balanced. We looked straight at each other, held our breath and finally laughed so hard we almost spit out some fish.

Chapter Sixteen
Monday, September 15, 1975, Henniker, New Hampshire

Sam called his boss first thing Monday to tell him he'd be late. He didn't have to go into a detailed explanation. That was one of the perks of working at New Sussex College in the small town of Henniker. People were very relaxed. Control freaks need not apply.

Sam had become known to all of the Henniker Police the year before. In this small New Hampshire town, Sam's pursuit of a Nazi war criminal hiding as a Biology professor had been big news.

Just after eight o'clock, Sam pulled up to the police station, walked in and saw Chief Cal Powers pouring a cup of coffee from the community pot. The small lobby with a desk officer received visitors. Separated from the desk area by a wooden railing, an access gate swung open.

When he walked into the station, the desk officer waved and gave him a smile. "Hiya, Sam. Funny to see you here first thing on Monday. You applying for a job?"

"Not today, Sergeant, just here to see the chief."

Chief Powers turned at the sound of Sam's voice and waved him in as he cradled the coffee cup and eased his way toward his office. Sam followed him into the chief's office a moment later, sliding into a wooden chair facing the chief's desk. Cal Powers had placed his coffee cup on the desk and sat in a new, high-back swivel chair behind it. "What's up, Sam? Want a coffee?"

"No thanks, Chief. I won't be long. I'd just like to ask you a favor."

Cal sipped his coffee with both hands gripping the warm cup. "Certainly, Sam. What can I help you with?"

"You've met Bart Sanborn and his partner, Auggie Raymond, I believe."

"Well, I was at the open house they held at Ocean Born Mary's, but we never actually got to talk much. Martha introduced me to her brother and pointed out Auggie Raymond. That's about it. Say, I hear they're stirring up a good business around that old legend."

Sam scratched his chin before replying. "Yeah, they've gotten off to a good start.

"Cal, I'm here because Martha asked me to talk to you. It's nothing big, but she has a bad feeling about her brother's partner, Auggie. She's known him since he and Bart became friends as kids, and she never liked him. She said he was a manipulator and often led Bart down a wrong path. She doesn't know if he's ever had any trouble with the law, but hopes you can check him out to see if he has an arrest record. That's all. I'm sorry to bother you with this, but you know how Martha can be, so . . ."

Chief Powers cut him off. "No need to apologize, Sam. I'll be glad to check him out for you. It will speed things up if you can give me more information about him: automobile make and tag number, previous address, his full name, stuff like that."

"Of course. I'll check with Martha about that and get back to you. Thanks, Cal."

"Glad to help, and I sure hope I come up with a zero on this fellow. The Ocean Born Mary legend can be a fun thing, but it could be something else if a con-man is involved. I'll get on this as soon as I've heard back from you."

The two shook hands, and Sam made his exit.

By Thursday, Sam was itching for a reply from Chief Powers. He wanted to have a face-to-face with Auggie, but needed more information about him. When the call came in from the chief, Sam was stunned.

Auggie was clean, with no arrests, complaints, or charges of any kind. Sam would have sworn that Auggie had some dirt on him somewhere, but the chief said he'd found nothing. Sam still wanted to talk to Auggie, but he wasn't sure what his approach would be. He'd just have to play it by ear.

A little deception can be helpful, whether playing cards or trying to survive in a hostile environment like Auschwitz, so Sam decided he should cover his tracks in trying to meet with Auggie. It was near quitting time when he buzzed Martha, asking her to call the house to find out if Bart and Auggie were there. He wanted to catch Auggie alone.

"Okay, Sam, what's going on?"

"You asked me to help out, so that's what I'm going to do." Sam revealed the plan to his lady friend.

"I'll make the call, but what do you want me to say if they are both there?"

"Just say that you wanted to chat with Bart. If he is there, make up some small talk, maybe about Teresa, since they appear to be interested in each other. You're family, so you are naturally curious."

"I can do that. I'll make the call right now and get back to you."

Fifteen minutes later, Sam got the news from Martha. Bart had left with Teresa, and Auggie was checking inventory in the gift shop. The timing looked good.

Within minutes, Sam had parked in front of the house and was within a few feet of the front door when it opened. Auggie emerged from the building, surprised to see Sam.

"If you're looking for Bart, he's not here. But I'll bet you knew that."

"Why do you say that?" Sam was caught off guard.

"Well, you work with Martha and are pretty close. She called here a few minutes ago asking for Bart. There's a chance you talked with her before coming over. Am I right?"

Sam thought Auggie was sharp. "Actually, I'm here to see you. It's nothing big, but I've never had a chance to talk to you without a group around. I thought maybe we could spend some time getting better acquainted. That's all."

"Fair enough, but I don't have a lot of time. I'm on my way over to the Historical Society, but I guess we can chat a while."

The two men moved away from the house, strolling toward the old well. It gave them something to lean on.

"Martha says you and Bart go way back and have been in on some enterprises before. How'd you think up this one?"

Auggie leaned back against the well wall and folded his arms. "We were talking one day, and it just popped into the conversation. We're both from New Hampshire, so we knew about the old legend. Bart said he thought the old place had been vacant for a long time, and the ghost legend used to be pretty popular. We talked about how people seem to love ghost stuff and were willing to let others separate them from their money. If it worked before for Allan Royston, then maybe it could work again. Lo and behold, here we are."

Sam thought about those words, "If it worked before it could work again." He thought of the Nazi war criminal he had found a year ago, and how he and others were trying to bring back the Reich. *Some things must never be brought back,* he thought.

"Good thing you two are single and don't have families to tie you down. It would have been hard to get your plan going with a wife and kids." Sam realized his words applied to himself.

"That's why I've stayed single. I need to be able to move on whenever I wish."

"What about your mom?"

"I've always tried to take care of her as best I can. We were living together, Mom and me, in Boston. Bart keeps in touch and came to me with this idea. As long as Mom could be in on it, I liked the idea. Bart knew that Royston used his mom in the old days, so he had no objections. Besides, having a grandmotherly figure in the house helps sell the place. That's better for business."

Sam was impressed with Auggie's self-assured manner.

"What other types of work have you done, Auggie? I mean, was this a whole new game for you, or did you have any similar experiences?"

Auggie stiffened up and paused. Sam figured he was getting annoyed with the questioning.

"I've done a lot of sales over the years, Sam. I used to sell sheetrock on the road. It took me all over New England. I met a lot of people in different types of places; cities, suburbs, small towns. I had to talk to people in groups and go one-on-one. It's all salesmanship, same as this."

"I see what you mean." Sam decided that Auggie was a drifter at heart and a momma's boy, to boot. *Chief Powers said he has a clean sheet, so there probably isn't anything to worry about.* He figured Martha was being overly protective of her brother. *This ghost house business might be a weak business concept, but Martha is worrying too much.*

Chapter Seventeen
Henniker, New Hampshire, September 9, 1950

Allan Royston had a tour of thirteen people moving through the Ocean Born Mary house on a warm and humid Saturday morning. He had them in the living room with the windows open to help capture an occasional breeze. Ghost stories are hard to tell when the audience is distracted by uncomfortable weather.

As far as Royston could tell, the tour group consisted of five couples in their twenties and thirties. as well as three young men in T-shirts and khaki pants. They had crew cut hair, and two of the young men wore black, army-style boots. Allan figured them to be recently discharged veterans who attended the young college that had been established after the war. They each sported an open beer bottle and were having no problem throwing them back at an early hour. They were well behaved, except for an occasional giggle fit.

"Come closer to the fireplace, everyone, and take note of this large and beautiful hearthstone. It holds great significance." Royston took a deep breath, as if about to start a great speech.

"What's it made out of, silver or something?" The young man chuckled, swigged his beer and glanced at his two friends, who joined him in a giggle.

"No, young man. It's just a big stone, typical of those found in New Hampshire, that was dug out by farmers who were clearing the land. But notice the cracks in the mortar around it. That tells us that it has not been resting in place. People have worked at moving it. Here's why."

The beer drinkers quieted down in anticipation.

Royston stepped up onto the hearthstone, which boosted him up about six inches, so he could be better seen by all. It was his stage.

"In 1788, Mary moved into this house at the age of sixty-four. It was a happy time in her life, and she enjoyed being with her family. A remarkable event took place, however, that she could never have expected. The very pirate who had attacked her mother's ship, Don Pedro, showed up at the house and introduced himself to Mary. He was in his eighties, well dressed and civilized. Mary was taken with him, and they saw each other often, eventually getting married. Don Pedro moved into the grand house with her."

Hushed voices rumbled through the room when the tour group heard mention of Don Pedro.

"How did she know it was really him?" asked one woman.

"He told her of her birth and his gift of green silk for her wedding gown. No one else living at that time could have known of this, so she was convinced he was the real Don Pedro."

Royston felt he had the audience in the palm of his hand.

"As the story goes, Mary arrived home one day after being in town. She was driving a horse and buggy by herself. She saw Don Pedro and another man carrying a large black chest to the orchard behind the house. She kept her suspicion to herself and never talked to him about it."

One of the beer drinkers blurted out, "Yo-ho-ho . . . eh . . . somethin' on a dead man's chest. Must have been the treasure, eh, matey?"

Royston didn't like being heckled, but he played along. "You're onto something, young man. Two years later, Mary arrived home at dusk, and as her horse became unsettled, she saw an old man fleeing the house. The man grabbed at his side and collapsed." Royston did his best to act out the scene.

"Mary ran into the house and found Don Pedro on the floor, bleeding badly from a stab wound. He told Mary about burying treasure in the orchard. The other man was an old shipmate who'd trailed Don Pedro to Henniker in hopes of grabbing the loot. The men were very old, but their pirate toughness and lust for treasure endured. The old pirates fought, and Don Pedro was stabbed. He managed to take the knife away from his attacker and stab him. The man knew he was no match for Don Pedro and tried to flee, but his wound was fatal, and he didn't get far."

The group was silent, mesmerized by the story. Even the college guys calmed down, swilling more beer while awaiting the rest of the story.

Royston paced across the hearth, enjoying the hold he had over his audience. "Don Pedro whispered his final words to Mary, and her eyes filled with tears as her second husband passed away."

"Mary enlisted her son to help her carry out Don Pedro's final instructions. They dug up the treasure and buried the pirate killed by Don Pedro. They cremated Don Pedro in a fire built away from the house. Then they brought his ashes and the treasure into the house. The Wallaces were wealthy and didn't need or want pirate loot, so they followed the dead pirate's instructions and buried it, along with his ashes, in a most secure place."

Royston paused to let that idea sink in, waiting to see if anybody got it. Hearing nothing from the group, he tapped his foot loudly on the hearthstone. "Yes. It's right here, under my foot."

There were gasps from the audience. One of the beer drinkers finally spoke. "Why doesn't somebody dig it up? Come on, get some tools and we can move that stone."

Royston broke into a grin. "I said that the treasure was in a secure place, didn't I? Well, let me tell you why. Mary keeps it that way. That's right, her ghost guards this treasure. Men have tried to dig it up and have paid the price for it. Once a storm blew while two men were in here trying to get at it. A window was shattered, sending a shard of glass into the eye of one of the thieves. They ran out screaming and were never seen again."

Groans came from the group.

"Just a few years back, a man broke in here and tried to force me to help him lift the stone. I told him it was too heavy and refused, so the stubborn man tried to lift it himself. I exaggerated the weight of the stone, and I believe that this man—who was young and healthy—could have done it, if he were careful and used the proper tools. But as he struggled with the stone, he grabbed at his chest and keeled over, dead of a heart attack. There was an account of the death in the local newspapers. You see, the ghost of Ocean Born Mary protects the house and all that's in it."

Most in the group seemed impressed with this tale. The beer drinkers seemed much less eager to move the stone. Royston felt he had struck sufficient fear in everyone, and they didn't call his bluff.

He took the group out of the house to let them inspect the orchard, and he made some final remarks to conclude the tour. Another group would assemble for the next tour, and Royston wanted to rest and wet his whistle before moving on. He was building his own treasure in the Ocean Born Mary house.

Chapter Eighteen
Tuesday, September 16, 1975, Henniker, New Hampshire

I was worried about Bart. His friendship with Auggie was looking less friendly, and I wanted to get a good picture of what was going on, so I went over to the house to see him during my lunch break. Maybe he saw me as just a nosy sister, but I was used to being pushy with men to get answers when I sought them. Of course, my relationship to these men usually wasn't of the brotherly type.

Auggie was in the dining room, sitting at the table and writing something on a notepad when I walked in. He gave me a polite smile. "If you're looking for Bart, he's outside in the back."

"Thanks, you're on target."

I found my brother pacing off some yardage, as if he was planning a building plot. "What gives, brother?"

He stopped and seemed surprised, like a child embarrassed to be caught at play. "I'm working on an idea, nothing fantastic. What gives with you?"

I plunked myself down at a picnic table. It was a picturesque early fall day, so an outdoor talk would be pleasant, as well as ensuring we would keep a safe distance from Auggie. Bart joined me, easing onto a seat across the table.

"I wanted to see how you were doing. You were pretty angry with Auggie, and I hope that is settled down. Believe it or not, I do want you guys to succeed in this venture, even if I think it is harebrained." I chuckled, hoping to ease the tension he might have felt. I couldn't tell if it worked.

"I appreciate your concern, but there's nothing to worry about. Auggie and I have arguments sometimes, sort of like siblings, you know?"

"Yeah, I get your point."

"Look, Auggie is smart, a good idea man, and I respect his ability to come up with ways to promote the business."

"Has he come up with any great ideas recently? So far, the best thing you've got going is Teresa, and she dropped into your laps."

"As a matter of fact, I was going to call you about something that we hope to do Thursday night. I've contacted a medium in Massachusetts, through a friend there. She's going to communicate with Ocean Born Mary in a séance. I was hoping you and Sam could take part. If it goes well, we might hire her to do it for members of the public. Maybe she could be featured on Halloween night."

"A séance?" I considered this for a moment. "Sounds like it could be cool. I've never done one of those. I think they're bullshit, of course, but it could be a fun experience."

"Maybe that's why you never took part in one."

"Figures, doesn't it? Okay, let's give it a go. This could be interesting."

He studied me for a moment before speaking. "You've got that look in your eye that tells me you're going to give her a hard time."

"Of course I am. She should be able to handle a little skepticism. Don't you think she's had that before and will again? Maybe on Halloween night, for instance?"

"Of course, you're right about that," he said quickly. "Like I said, she'll be here Thursday night. I'll confirm the time with Auggie and let you know. Ocean Born Mary will be pleased to meet you."

I started to get up but stopped and sat back down. "What about Teresa? I hope she'll be there. I'm sure she'll want to speak to her great, great, great—say, how many greats does she have between her and Mary?"

"I don't know," said Bart, counting with his fingers. "We'll have to check with her or Monty. Yes, he'll be invited, too. Should be a fine party."

I tried to recall the words to a song that Sinatra and Crosby sang in the movie, *High Society*.

Have you heard, it's in the stars,
Next July we collide with Mars,
Well, did you ever?
What a swell party this is.

I couldn't wait for Thursday night. Watching the clock was a real problem for me all day at work. *What a slow day.*

Sam agreed to have dinner with me at my house, and we decided to make it quick and simple. Sam picked up a roasted chicken from the market, while I went ahead home to cook some rice and heat a can of vegetables.

We sat at the kitchen table and worked on a red wine. I was all excited, but Sam seemed to be drifting away. I couldn't understand his lack of enthusiasm at first, but then it came to me. He was having what I often thought of as a *Carol Vasile Day*.

Maybe I can shake him out of it.

"I know I'm a skeptic, but I'm excited about finally experiencing something like this, and I'm going to make a real effort to be open-minded. I swear I am. You know, maybe there is something about this idea of communicating with the dead. Maybe you should ask her about your mom. What do you think?"

Sam was looking away from the table as I spoke. Maybe he was already searching for a link to somebody, but not a dead person. His eyes shot back to me, however, as soon as I mentioned his mom.

"You aren't really starting to believe in that stuff now, are you? I believe that if Mom could talk to me, she would have by now."

"You're probably right, but neither of us has ever been to a séance before, correct? Maybe there's something to it we've never thought of."

Sam sipped some wine as I stared into his eyes. He waited a moment before speaking. "We all have dead loved ones we'd like to communicate with. These mediums know that and take advantage of our emotions."

"I agree with that, but I'm trying to lighten up a little, just for tonight. Can you try to do that too, Sam?"

"Okay, I'll try. Maybe I've got a challenge for this woman."

"Besides trying to contact your mother, Sadie? She's been dead for a long time. It seems to me that is quite a challenge by itself."

Sam put his glass down and rested his elbows on the table, folding his hands together. "I wonder if she can contact a living person, someone who is far away?"

"You mean Carol, don't you? I felt that you had her on your mind. Yeah, that would be interesting, a medium who could contact the long-lost living." I felt my eyes starting to water, so I got up and took my plate to the sink before Sam could detect me slipping.

It wasn't supposed to happen this way. We were supposed to be friends with benefits, but I needed this man more and more. It became evident to me whenever he talked about Carol.

"I didn't mean to bother you, Martha. Sorry."

I stood at the sink, my back to Sam, and suppressed a sniffle. *Bad girl, Martha. Grow up!*

I pulled myself together and got back into *good old Martha* mode. We drove to the house just before seven and found Bart, Auggie and Lucy in the dining room. They were drinking wine with a short, blonde woman I didn't know. Soft classical music played from somewhere.

Bart flipped on his charm switch and hustled over to me as we entered. "Ah, just the person I was waiting for.

Martha, I want to introduce you to Willa von Schrenck, our medium. She'll be conducting the séance tonight."

She was very small and fragile looking, with long hair and bright blue eyes. She bore a striking resemblance to Teresa, except for the eye color; she could have passed for her little sister.

"Hello, Martha. I'm very glad to meet you. Bart has told me a great deal about you and Sam, who must be the handsome gentleman next to you."

She didn't waste time. Her eyes surveyed Sam from head to foot, and she edged closer to him, extending her hand. Sam played nice and gave it a gentle shake. I moved in, forcing my body against Sam's side and smiling hard. *Von Schrenck my ass. Where's the accent? She's probably Sue Smith from South Boston or something.*

"That's an interesting name," said Sam.

"Yes, Bavarian," she cooed. "But, to be honest, I don't know much about it. It's really like a stage name that I use professionally. I believe it adds some mystery, don't you think?"

I knew it. Sam gave a soft laugh, and Bart joined him. *Remember, girl, you're going to be nice and keep an open mind. It's going to be tough.*

The sound of footsteps caused everyone to turn around, and we watched Teresa and Monty make their entrance from the hall. Monty looked handsome and dignified, as usual. Teresa looked absolutely stunning in a flowing yellow dress that was cut low at the top. Even our medium couldn't help but stare. I stifled a yawn as the new members of the party were introduced.

"Let's get started, folks," said Bart. "The spirit world awaits us. Willa is going to arrange our seating."

She moved to a seat with the fireplace directly behind her, and Bart pulled a chair out for her. She proceeded to direct everyone to their seats, and I thought it was cute the way she made it a boy-girl-boy-girl set up. *I should have guessed.*

She waited until we all were seated before sliding into hers. She placed her hands on the table and nodded to Bart, who was seated next to her.

"Excuse me, folks, but since this is a rehearsal of sorts, I'm going to be giving Willa some assistance that she wouldn't normally get from a guest at the table. Please, hold on."

Bart disappeared into the passageway to the kitchen, and in a moment the music faded and the light over the table dimmed. Bart reentered the room and reclaimed his seat. I guess the dimmer switch was in the kitchen, along with controls for the music system.

Willa began with instructions to the group. She asked us to place our hands on the table and take hold of the hands of our neighbors. Bart was to my left and Sam to my right. I glanced at Sam, and he winked at me. I turned toward Bart, but he stared straight ahead, paying no attention to me. *Is he really getting into it, or is he part of the act? Is there an act?*

"We are going to seek out Mary and bring her spirit to us. Remember, if she appears to us, that is her choice. We cannot compel her to appear, but if we are willing and receptive, perhaps she will sense our positive energy and grant us a visit. So please, hold your neighbor's hand gently, close your eyes for a moment and think of Mary. Tell her, in your mind, that you believe she is here and you wish to communicate with her. I will tell you when to open your eyes. Thank you." Her voice was soft, but assertive.

Okay, Martha, be a good girl. Give this thing a shot.

I squeezed my eyes shut and hoped Sam was doing the same. The room was nearly silent aside from the sound of breathing. After a minute or so, Willa spoke.

"You can open your eyes now, but please do not speak. Remain very quiet. I feel the energy growing in the room."

I opened my lids and looked around. Everyone but Willa and Bart did the same. They looked straight ahead.

As I turned my head about, I saw something that caught my attention. There was an old wooden rocking chair near the wall behind Willa. It seemed to rock without any noise. It stopped and then moved again. I gripped Sam's hand and nodded toward the chair. He got my message and squeezed back, acknowledging me. Monty stiffened in his chair as he witnessed the same motion. Everyone except Bart and Willa looked at the chair momentarily.

"I'm feeling a strong presence," said Willa. "Yes. It's getting stronger. It's a man."

Teresa gave a short yipping sound and dipped her right shoulder as if she felt pressure there. Everyone looked at her. She looked startled. *Is she in on it too?*

"Everything is all right, Teresa. Just relax." Willa's words calmed the woman, but only for a moment.

Teresa opened her mouth, and I heard a soft gasp. Her head turned to one side, as if she was responding to a touch. She repeated the motion to the other side, and her eyes opened wide. We sat motionless. I was conflicted. I wanted to believe what I was witnessing was real, but I couldn't shake the idea that it was an act.

If it was an act, it was a very good one. Teresa suddenly broke the hand holds and stood up. Her arms fell to her sides, and her face was drawn. I scanned the table to catch other reactions. Monty looked stunned, as did Auggie. Lucy's eyes darted about the room, also searching for reactions. Then came the stunner.

"There is a woman present also," said Willa. "She is troubled."

I was still holding Bart and Sam's hands when Teresa spoke. Her voice sounded hollow and gravelly. *"No let her go, she's not the one. The Mary of your youth is long gone. You can never get her back."*

I didn't know what to make of it as I watched Teresa go limp and slump into her chair. Monty reached for her, guiding her onto the seat.

Willa jumped up as Teresa sat. "Are you okay, Teresa? Can you speak?"

Sam and I glanced at each other. His face showed a slight grin, while I shook my head. Other than Willa and Teresa, everyone remained quiet. Were they being good actors? Bart broke the spell and rushed to Teresa, taking her hand and kneeling beside her.

While most everyone was focused on Teresa, I saw Lucy nudge her son with an elbow and question him. "I thought this was a rehearsal, you know, the stuff we went over. So what's with the improv?"

Auggie waved his mother off and kept his eyes on Bart and Teresa.

I was amused by the question. *Seems like somebody is trying to steal the show.*

I beckoned Sam with my index finger, and he leaned toward me, offering an ear. "Bart looks really concerned. What do you make of this?"

It was my turn to give an ear to Sam, and our heads shifted accordingly. "Too early to tell. Let it play out."

I nodded, and my eyes went back to Bart, who was clutching Teresa's left hand with both of his. He began rubbing her hand. "Are you okay, dear? Can you talk?"

She opened her eyes, as if just waking from a deep sleep, and surveyed the dim room. She seemed surprised to find Bart kneeling at her side. "Bart, what happened? Why is everyone staring at me?"

Bart's eyes went around the room, confirming Teresa's assertion.

I leaned forward and joined the conversation. "Teresa, you blacked out for a moment. Do you remember what happened just before that?" Bart looked at me and nodded, as if to say he had the same question.

"No, I don't know, exactly," she said. She sat up in her chair and rubbed her forehead with her right hand. Bart still had a claim on her left. "Willa said something about a man being present but that's all I remember. Everything is blank after that."

I turned back to Willa when she spoke. "Bart." She pointed to the overhead light, and Bart got the message. He broke from Teresa long enough to leave the room. The light went to full brightness, and he returned to Teresa's left side. She assured him she felt okay, and Bart returned to his seat.

Willa reclaimed control of the program. "What you all saw here tonight was a confirmation that others reside in this great house. Ocean Born Mary spoke to us through Teresa."

"That makes sense to me," added Monty. "Teresa is Mary's direct descendent. She's a logical conduit for Mary."

Lucy blurted out something unintelligible to me, and Auggie cut her off. I smiled as he patted her arm.

"No, no, Mom, it's okay. I like this. It's very good, and very convincing. Bart, old boy, you've outdone yourself. I've never seen you show such creativity. Well done, well done."

I wasn't satisfied. "What about the man, Willa? You said you felt his presence first. So where did he go? I didn't hear a toilet flush, so I don't think he took a potty break."

Willa didn't skip a beat, looking straight at me. "Did you listen to what Mary said through Teresa? She was talking to him. The voice said that the Mary of his youth was gone."

Monty jumped back in. "Yes, the pirate's girlfriend—er, fiancée had died, and he was reminded of her by the newborn baby with green eyes."

It was Auggie's turn. "And that baby grew up to look like, well, Teresa. I like it."

I noticed that Bart remained quiet and stared at Teresa. She returned his look for a moment and then diverted her eyes.

I guess Monty had had enough. He got up and declared the event a success. "I've attended several of these types of events over the years, even one held right here by Allan Royston, many years ago. But I've never seen anything as convincing and genuine as this. I was sitting right next to her the whole time, and I swear that voice came out of her mouth. I see no sign of a gimmick anywhere—no wires, no hidden speaker. Miss von Schrenck, you have my admiration. And with that, I'm going to bid you all goodnight."

Auggie and I were the only ones to return his courtesy. The others looked like they didn't care if he stayed or went.

I turned toward Bart on my left and touched his arm. "What do you think? Was this a success?"

Bart was hesitant. "Yes, I guess I'd have to say so. If the general public was here tonight, I think they'd have gotten their money's worth. That's what we're here for, right everybody?"

"Damned right, partner, damned right." Auggie's voice raised the decibel level. "I admit you caught me off guard for a minute, Bart, but I don't mind. This was a great show. It's going to be a big success. I can't wait for Halloween."

Sam was seated with his arms across his chest. I could see the wheels spinning in his head, as if he was gearing up for a question. I was right.

"Willa, what time did you arrive here?" Sam asked.

"I was here just before three o'clock. Why do you ask?"

"And you had a dry run of sorts, a rehearsal for the rehearsal, I guess?"

"Yes. Me, Bart, Auggie and his mom. We had to make sure we were all on the same page about some things." Willa was not ruffled by Sam's questions.

"So, Teresa and Monty were not part of that dry run."

"That's correct. I understand your questioning, Sam, and it's perfectly understandable. No, Teresa was not putting on an act. What you saw here tonight was absolutely genuine. Ocean Born Mary was with us in this room, speaking through Teresa." Willa spoke with the confidence of a competitor who had just brought home a victory.

Chapter Nineteen
Henniker, New Hampshire, 1953

Abigail Royston served a bowl of hot, homemade soup to her son in the kitchen of the old house he had bought many years before. The big, rustic kitchen had a huge fireplace where Mary Wallace had prepared many a meal for her own son after she had come to live there. But Abigail had insisted on a modern gas range, fueled by two large propane tanks beside the house. Her son was glad to oblige her and benefitted from his mother's fine cooking. She was getting along in years, however, and he knew the day would come when he'd be on his own.

"Thank you, Mother," he said as he stirred the hot soup to cool it. "You've always been a big help to me." He added some crackers to the meal as Abigail served herself and sat across from him at the table.

"Allan, it's time we talked about your future. I'm not getting any younger and, for that matter, neither are you. It's been a great deal of fun living in this grand old house and working the business, but you know that we are losing money here. The old legend isn't as popular as it used to be. This is a new age, Allan. People would rather watch things on television than go out at night. Ocean Born Mary can't compete with Milton Berle. I'll be gone one day, and you need to plan for that time. You need to have money in the bank and be ready for your own late years. They'll come upon you faster than you think."

Allan spooned soup into his mouth without looking at his mother. He knew her words were true, but he hated thinking about that time when she would no longer be there to help him and share in the fun of keeping Ocean Born Mary alive.

"Oh, Mother, you're not going anywhere for a long time. We've got years to look forward to. There's much more excitement ahead for us and Mary. You'll see. The soup is terrific, Mother."

"There you go," she replied. "You're always the optimist. I love that about you, Allan, but sometimes you have to be practical. You'll need to make your own soup someday."

The future that Allan and his mother talked about shrank to months as the winter of 1954 became too harsh for her old body to take. Arthritis made it difficult for her to do chores, work the business and climb stairs. Her son would never spend the money needed to install central heating, preferring to use the old fireplaces. The house lacked modern insulation and couldn't hold fireplace heat very efficiently. The net result was a quick decline in Abigail's health.

In April of that year, Abigail contracted pneumonia, and her warning to Allan proved to be true. He was on his own.

Royston insisted on keeping his mother close to him, so he shoveled out a grave for her in the corner of the lot near the tree line. It was visible from his bedroom window. Her obituary ran in the local newspaper, but no service was held.

A few days after the obituary ran, Allan received a surprise visitor. He answered a knock on the front door, and a young man whom he hadn't seen in years greeted him.

"Hello, Uncle Roy. I hope you are well. I read about Grandmother's death, and wanted to pay my respects. I hope that's okay."

Seth Proctor was the son of Allan's long-dead sister. He lived in Manchester, but the two were never close. Seth thought his uncle, whom he called Uncle Roy, was either a crackpot or a fraud, and after one exposure to an Ocean Born Mary house event, he'd decided to keep his distance.

"Yes, yes, that's okay, Seth. Thank you for coming. Please come in."

Their greeting was pleasant, and Allan served coffee in the dining room. They sat at the round table where many a visitor had come to communicate with the ghost of Mary. "I'd offer you something to eat, but I'm not much of a cook. I always relied on Mother."

"That's not necessary, Uncle, but thank you. Now that she's gone, I'm sorry that I didn't visit Grandmother very much."

"She would have liked that, but you had your reasons. I'm not angry about it. You have your own family to take care of."

"How are you getting along? Will you still operate your business?"

"I'm okay, Seth. I can pay off the mortgage and stay here. I can handle the taxes and do my best to keep up the property. I want to live here until I join Mother. As for the business, I'm afraid that's at an end. Mother and I spoke about it last fall, and she was right. There is little interest in a ghost legend today. Oh, I'm sure some of the college crowd will get drunk and show up on Halloween, but I'll shoo them away. No more shows."

Seth sipped his coffee, set the cup on the table and glanced around. "It's a fine old house, Uncle. You restored it very well over the years."

Allan stared at his nephew, wondering if there was something more he wanted to ask about. After a pause, Seth looked up and smiled at his uncle.

"Thanks for the coffee. I'd better be going."

Allan walked Seth to the door and watched him trot back to his car. The vehicle sped off, and Allan closed the door.

Noticing a chill in the air, he grabbed a jacket and strode outside to Abigail's grave. He felt a visit was in order.

"Had a surprise visit today, Mother. Seth stopped by. He said he wanted to pay his respects. Imagine that. He didn't have much respect for us all these years, but I guess death has a way of bringing family together, for whatever reason. Maybe he's got an eye for the place, I don't know for sure, or maybe he's just doing the right thing for his grandmother. Maybe it's as simple as that."

As the years went by, Allan lapsed into depression, and liquor became his companion. He ate very little, never obtaining the kitchen skills of his mother. On a typical evening, he kindled a fire in the living room and settled into an easy chair with a glass of whiskey.

"Hello, Old Mr. Boston," he said admiring his glass. "I'm old Mr. Henniker. How nice to see you again." He swallowed a sip and set the glass down on the table next to him. "You know, you've been a good buddy over the years. Really, since Mother's been gone, you're the only one who seems to care. I wish she would talk to me. She could at least do that. Mary does. Good old Mary. I still catch a glimpse of her. I guess she doesn't see me, but I see her, that old ghost girl." He took a bigger swallow of whiskey.

"Someday, Mary, you'll have somebody else keeping you company in this house. Question is, who? Who's gonna be crazy enough to buy this old hunk of wood, like I did? Hey, I've got an idea. Maybe I'll leave it to that nephew of mine in Manchester. What's his name? I saw him a few years back. Could've sworn he was going to ask me about it. Well, maybe he won't have to ask. Maybe I'll just leave it to him. What the hell? He is family, after all. Won't he be tickled! Course, kid, you got to wait 'til I croak. Hah."

Allan Royston lived for several more years, allowing both the property and his health to decline. Night after night, he held a fireside chat with his buddy in a glass. The routine took a toll on his liver and stomach, and in 1965 they had had enough, as had his heart.

Seth Proctor was quite surprised when he got the lawyer's call about his uncle's will. Both pleased and puzzled, he wasn't sure what to make of it. According to the provisions of the will, he could sell off the majority of the acreage, but the house had to remain on a parcel of two acres. The Ocean Born Mary house was to stand for as long as nature allowed. The ghostly resident would always have her home.

Part Two

Chapter Twenty

Thursday, September 18, 1975, Henniker, New Hampshire

I couldn't believe my ears. I squeezed the phone receiver as I sat up on my bed and swung my legs over the side, planting my feet on the floor.

"Sam, what are you telling me? This is crazy. Auggie is dead, and Bart's been arrested for murder? We were there just a couple of hours ago." My head began to ache, like it does when I don't get enough sleep. My alarm clock said one-twenty-five a.m. My concentration was being tested as I listened to Sam.

"I'm coming right over, Martha. Be there in a few minutes."

A few minutes didn't give me much time for freshening up, but I did my best to put on a face, slosh some mouthwash and slide into jeans and a pullover sweatshirt. Sneakers without socks would do.

There was leftover coffee in the pot, so I heated that up and fixed a cup for myself. There'd be some left for Sam. I paced the kitchen, clutching the cup with both hands. *Holy shit. What is going on?*

The sound of a car door closing told me to unlock my front door. I opened it as Sam was jogging up the walkway and into my arms. I pulled him inside and closed the front door.

"Jesus, Sam, tell me what's happening. Wait, I've got to get my coffee. You want some?"

He followed me into the kitchen without answering and went right to the cabinet for a cup. Sam motioned toward the table, and we grabbed chairs, slid into them and angled next to each other.

"Chief Powers called me. He figured Bart wouldn't be contacting you any time soon, and he felt we should know right away. I guess he felt more comfortable calling me, knowing I'd bring you the news. It's not good."

"What did he say? What happened?" I put my cup on the table and palmed Sam's chest with both hands.

"Cal told me that Lucy called the police from the house. She said Auggie was lying on the kitchen floor in a pool of blood, and Bart was kneeling next to him with a gun in his hands. She ran upstairs screaming, locked herself in her room and made the call. That's all Cal would tell me. He told me not to go over to the house. Bart was arrested and booked at the police station, but sheriff's deputies were taking him to the new county jail in Boscawen."

I jumped from my seat. "Well, all right then, let's go there."

Sam shook his head.

"What? We've got to go, Sam. Bart needs me." But Sam didn't budge from his seat.

"No, hon, I'm afraid we can't. I asked Cal if we could do that, and he said no. It's after midnight, so this is Friday. Arraignment comes a business day after the arrest, and you can't see a prisoner until sometime after the arraignment. We won't get to see him until next week."

"What?"

Sam tried to ease me back into my chair, but I pulled away.

"You mean I can't even talk to him? What about his one phone call? Maybe he'll call me."

"No, Martha, this isn't a movie. That's just a Hollywood thing. I think the best we can do is get him a lawyer. Maybe he can get in. Do you know a lawyer?"

"Oh, shit, you got to be kidding me! I'm his sister, and you're telling me I can't see him?" I spun around as if looking for an escape route, but there was no place to go.

Sam repeated his question.

"Yeah, I know a guy in Concord: Harry Parsons. He's originally from Henniker. We dated a few times, you know."

Sam understood.

"I'll call him right now."

Sam nodded. It was late, but I had to do something to help Bart. Sam stood up and took me in his arms. The warmth of his hug was calming and helped a lot.

Harry wasn't too pleased to get my call in the middle of the night, but he was accustomed to such experiences from clients. I hadn't been in touch with him for several years, and he avoided making small talk, for which I was grateful. I was sure he didn't want this to sound like a social call from a woman in the middle of the night, especially a woman he was familiar with. You might say *very* familiar at one time.

I made the story as brief as possible, and Harry promised to see Bart right away. It was reassuring to know that my brother would have a friendly visitor. Harry would get the details from Bart, and I'd meet him in his Concord office the next morning.

Sleep will be scarce tonight. Thank goodness I have Sam. When I finished my call to Harry, I went right to Sam's arms. He engulfed me in them. It was a good thing, for I felt like I was going to keel over without him holding me. I sobbed into his shirt.

Looking up at Sam, I struggled to get words out. "How can this be happening? Auggie is dead, and Bart is in jail. It doesn't seem real."

His arms were firm around me. For a minute, I felt a twinge of nausea, but it passed without calamity. My head was spinning like I had a whirlwind inside it.

Sam's hand caressed the back of my head, and he held it to his chest, my cheek turned into him. "Try to relax, sweetheart. I'm with you. Maybe you should have something stronger than coffee. I'll get us some wine."

"No, make mine whiskey," I said. "I need the heavy artillery."

"Got it. Two bourbons, coming right up."

He guided me to the living room sofa and eased me onto it. In a minute, Sam was back with drinks in each hand. I clutched mine as he passed it to me, my hands surrounding the highball glass. *Do your thing, Jim Beam.*

"Is this lawyer any good?" Sam asked as I sipped my medicine.

"I don't really know, come to think of it. I mean, I guess he's good, because he went from a cubbyhole office in Henniker to a nice one in a business building in Concord. But I don't even know if he's a trial lawyer or what. I guess I'll find out. He's the only attorney I know. He's going to see Bart as soon as he can, so that's a good start. The poor guy, he must be scared shitless."

I was taking bigger sips from my drink than I normally would, and before I knew it I was ready for a second. Sam was only halfway through his, but he refreshed mine and joined me on the sofa.

"Our boss is in for a shocker when I call in for both of us," said Sam. "It won't take long for word to get around town about Auggie."

"Oh shit, that's right. I'll have to call Teresa and tell her not to go to the house." I started to get up, but Sam held me back.

"That can wait until early morning. Might as well let her get a decent sleep tonight. No point in more people having insomnia."

His words made sense, so I dropped back onto the sofa with him. The bourbon began to help, giving me a slight buzz. Sam's hand caressing my hair was a bigger help.

Chapter Twenty-One
Friday Morning, September 19, 1975

I slept better than I had expected to, but I still felt like I had to lift a heavy load off my chest just to get out of bed. We slept in the nude, as usual, but making love was out of the question. I enjoyed the sight of him sleeping in my bed as I sat up and rested on my elbows.

What is this feeling he gives me? Is it security? Damn, I hate that word, but I'm sure glad he is in my life right now.

I made a slow rise off the bed, wove my way to the bathroom and did my early morning routine. By the time I was finished and getting dressed, Sam had gotten up, and I heard his voice from downstairs. He was on the phone. I hoped he was calling Teresa Thurgood. *Thanks, Sam. I don't want to explain things to her.*

He was off the phone and scrambling some eggs when I made my way into the kitchen. Bacon was sizzling on the stove. *What a great smell.*

"I tried calling Teresa to give her the news, but there was no answer," said Sam.

"Just as well, Sam. This is no party we're going to, and it has to be private."

"I'll call Bob Hill after we've eaten," said Sam. "Guess I should get him at home too, before he leaves for the library."

Sam already had his coffee, so I poured myself a cup and sat at the table. There was no banter during breakfast, no jovial chitchat. Time dragged like I was in a dentist's chair.

Sam made the call to our boss, while I went upstairs to brush my teeth. *What a way to start the day, dropping a bomb on someone.* Bob had gone through it before, when our college president was murdered. This was a lesser shock for him, so I knew he could handle it okay.

When I got back to the kitchen I reclaimed my seat at the table. "I'm struggling to figure this out, but I can't. Bart and Auggie have fought many times before, but like siblings, you know? They argue over the littlest thing and then make up. Bart's even threatened Auggie before, but it was always hollow. He never meant it." I shook my head, as if it would help.

"Maybe this time they fought for real." Sam's voice was matter-of-fact, and it stunned me. "This is a big money deal for them, and Bart's probably worried, since he put up the down payment cash. Or maybe it has to do with Teresa? Bart's taken a real liking to her, maybe more. Maybe he's fallen in love with her. If Auggie said something negative about her, he could have set Bart off. Who knows? Love or money have been motives for murder before."

"You can't think Bart murdered Auggie! At worst, it had to be an accident, something like that."

"No, I didn't mean to suggest Bart committed murder. I'm just saying that those two factors have led to serious conflicts throughout history. We'll know a lot more soon enough."

Soon? Bad word choice. If only there was some way to speed up the clock. I almost refilled my coffee but decided against it, figuring my bladder would turn into a weakling on me. I stopped Sam from cleaning the breakfast dishes so I could have a time-killing task. I moved as slowly as I could, but still only took about eight minutes. We wouldn't see Harry until nine.

As we finally made the drive to Concord, I sat in the passenger seat and gazed out on the fall landscape along Route 202. The beauty all around was lost on me, and I couldn't make good small talk. Sam flicked on the radio and got a local FM station, but I couldn't appreciate whatever was playing.

There were enough curbside parking spaces on Main Street, and Sam had no trouble easing into one a half block from Harry's law office. The lobby had a directory that showed Harry's office on the second floor. Taking the elevator was an easy choice.

A receptionist occupied a desk guarding a door to an inner office. She was younger than I expected; a stunningly good-looking kid with jet black hair and the natural equipment any lawyer named Harry could appreciate. *That's my Harry.*

"Hi, I'm Susan. You must be Martha Sanborn."

I nodded and extended my hand, which she shook politely. "Yes, and this is Sam Miller."

"Nice to meet you both. I'll let Harry know you are here."

She rose and seemed to glide to the door. Her dark blue dress was snug, emphasizing her figure, and was cut just above the knee, exposing the perfect amount of leg. *Did I look that good when I dated Harry?*

As she entered Harry's inner office, my look turned to Sam. His eyes were on me. Most guys would have popped their sockets on Susan, but Sam knew how to make a girl feel appreciated. I grinned and reached for his arm, squeezing it in acknowledgement.

Susan reappeared and ushered us in before returning to her desk. My old lover eased up from his chair to greet us. He was about Sam's height and had gained a little weight since I'd seen him last, but he still looked like he could move around a dance floor.

"Martha, Martha, wonderful to see you." He greeted me, his long arms circling me and almost lifting me off my feet in a gentle bear hug. We exchanged quick cheek kisses.

"Hello, Sam. A pleasure, considering the circumstances. Let's get right to it, shall we?"

Harry motioned us to a small, round table with four padded chairs. A file folder lay closed on the table where Harry took a seat. Sam and I took places beside each other, me close to Harry.

"How's Bart doing, Harry? I'm so grateful you were able to see him."

Harry spoke as he opened the file folder. A couple of typed papers were in it. "I had Susan type up my notes this morning. She's better at reading my scrawl than I am, so I prefer having them typed before I have to use them. Bart was in rough shape when I got there, scared and confused. But he calmed down enough to give me a good account of what had happened, as well as he could make of it."

"So he told you about the business that he and Auggie had started?"

"Yeah, I got the picture. Hard to believe that anyone would try blowing life into that old Ocean Born Mary legend, but heck, maybe the time is right for it. Sounds like they were making a good go of it." Harry fingered the papers in front of him.

I was anxious to hear Bart's story, and Harry could see that on my face.

"Okay, Bart said that he staged this séance as a rehearsal for a public one that would follow. He told me who was there and how it went. After everyone else had left, he and Auggie had a talk that grew into an argument. He said it had to do with money and a woman named Teresa, who had worked her way into the business."

"Yes, she just showed up one day and claimed to be a long lost descendent of Ocean Born Mary," I told Harry. "But her story passed scrutiny, and Bart took a liking to her."

"That's what he told me," said Harry. "Anyway, to move it along, Bart said Auggie started bitching about money. He thought they were paying the medium too much for the séance and some other things. It escalated, and he eventually griped that he wasn't pleased with how they shared the business. He felt that he was doing more work than what was in the original agreement, and he wanted a greater share. Bart provided the start up cash and, of course, didn't agree. He told me that they were shouting at each other, and it got pretty heated. He said they had both been drinking, and maybe that helped fuel the flames. But they calmed down and made up before Bart left."

"Bart left? But he lives there. Are you sure that's what he said?" I guess he could have left for any reason, but I thought it odd.

"Yes, he said he was going to see Teresa. He wanted to make sure she was okay after her experience at the séance. When he got to her place, he knocked, but there was no answer, so he went back to the house. This is when it gets interesting."

I didn't like the sound of that, and glanced at Sam. Our eyes met. He was calm, but I felt myself trembling. I looked back to Harry, and my silence told him to go on.

"Bart entered through the back door into the kitchen and found Auggie lying in a pool of blood. There was a small gun beside him on the floor. Bart assumed he was dead, but didn't touch him. He was shocked, and didn't know what to do. Unfortunately, for reasons he can't explain, Bart grabbed the gun. At that time, Auggie's mother appeared in the kitchen. She saw her son, apparently dead on the floor, and Bart holding a gun. She screamed, and that's when Bart noticed her. He said she kept screaming as she ran up the stairs. He was going to chase after her, but he stopped when he heard Auggie groan. Realizing Auggie was still alive, Bart tried to help him, pressing on the wound in an attempt to stop the bleeding. He asked Auggie who did this, but Auggie couldn't talk."

Harry stopped for a moment to catch his breath, and he looked at me for a reaction, but I didn't have any words.

The story was unfolding like a Hollywood murder mystery, unlike anything I could have imagined. Harry continued.

"Bart said he was overwhelmed and didn't know what else to do, so he decided to call for help. He got to the phone book on the kitchen counter, called the Henniker emergency number and told them he needed an ambulance. This took a couple of minutes, and Bart thinks that's when Auggie died. In a short time, the police arrived, but not the ambulance. I suggested to Bart that Auggie's mom probably made a call to the police before he made his emergency call. Anyway, the police arrested and cuffed Bart. Auggie's mother came downstairs and screamed at the police, 'He killed my son! He killed my son!' An officer tried to calm her down as Bart was led to a patrol car and taken away. So now he's in the county lockup."

"Harry, I've got to see him. When can I go there?"

"It could be days, or more likely a week. I'm sorry, but that's the way it is."

"But what am I supposed to do?"

"There's not much you can do, Martha. I suggest you let Sam take you home. I'll see Bart again today, and I also want to see this Teresa woman. I want to see Auggie's mother as well, if she's in any condition to talk."

"So you're going to take the case and defend Bart? If not, will you recommend somebody?" I didn't know what kind of a track record Harry had as a defense lawyer, if any, but I felt that I could trust him.

"To be frank, this doesn't look good for Bart. I need to know more about the circumstances—you know, who else might have something against Auggie, that sort of thing. That includes everyone at the séance. There was a fellow named Monty Phillips, so he's on my list too. I want to talk to you and Sam again, but I'm due in court soon, so it will have to wait. In the meantime, go over the events yourselves and see if you can come up with anything that might help. Okay? And get some rest."

"Okay, Harry. We'll do that." I looked at Sam, and he nodded agreement. "Rest sounds good, but I don't think I'll get any. This is just too unbelievable."

Chapter Twenty-Two

Friday, September 19, 1975, Henniker, New Hampshire

I never knew a twenty-minute drive could seem like a lifetime, but the ride home from Concord felt that way. *Who could have done this? Is there more to Teresa than we know? Does Monty know anything? What about Lucy? Is she putting on an act?* My head was spinning.

It was only around ten-thirty when we got back to my place. It was as if time had been suspended. It reminded me of when Kennedy was assassinated, and the world seemed to stand still for four days. For me, this was worse. This was my own flesh and blood who had been accused of murder. My stomach hurt.

Sam offered to make fresh coffee, and I decided that was a good idea. I would have liked something stronger, but it was way too early, even for me. There was a box of day old donuts in the fridge that would work as dunking fodder, so I got it out and put it on the table while Sam made the coffee.

"I'm going to make it decaf. I don't think we need any more stimulation. Agreed?"

Sam is such a sensible guy. "Agreed," I said as I eased into a chair, pulled a napkin from the holder on the table and selected a chocolate donut from the box. I couldn't wait for the drip coffee maker to do its work, so I pulled a small piece of donut and chucked it into my mouth. Sam put the milk and sweetener on the table, along with mugs and spoons. *What a feast.*

Sam poured coffee for both of us, and we settled in at the table.

"What did you think of Harry?" I asked. "Did he seem okay to you?"

"Honestly? I was impressed. He was more than I expected. I thought he did a good job with Bart, especially when you consider that he responded to a late call that was totally out of the blue for him. He never did say what his experience was as a defense attorney, but I think he's done some work in that arena. I like him."

"That makes me feel better, Sam. I respect your judgment. I feel good about Harry, too. I hope he stays on the case."

Sipping coffee, dunking a donut, talking with Sam, it all helped settle my belly. This man had changed my life, even if his heart was someplace else. Still, he had enough affection for me and kept me satisfied in more ways than one. I needed him.

We caught ourselves staring at each other, and I reached across the table for his arm. "I need you to help me with this."

"Of course, hon. I'm here for you."

"No, really, Sam, I mean it. You're steadier than I am. Look at everything you've been through, ever since you were a kid. I can't imagine what it must have been like at Auschwitz for you and your mother. Then, to have it all come back to you with that monster, Arthur Vasile, right here in Henniker. He was going to kill you, along with Carol and your friend, Eli. But you were strong, real strong. I need that kind of strength now. You've got to help me find out what happened. Promise me, please!"

Sam leaned toward me and clutched my hands. "I promise. You know I do."

He reached for my face and gave my cheek a warm caress. His words and his touch were like electricity surging through my body.

"Let's start right now," he said, withdrawing his hand and sitting up straight, as if convening a meeting. "We know the characters in this play, so let's go through them, one by one. Okay?"

"Okay," I said. "Shall we start with Auggie?"

"No. Let's start with Bart."

I was stunned by the sudden coldness in Sam's tone, but I took a breath and agreed. He was showing the steady strength that I had just asked for.

"He's the prime suspect, Martha, so let's look at the circumstances as objectively as possible to rule him out. Do you have a notepad we can use?"

That idea made perfect sense to me, so I got a pad and pen for Sam and dove in. "Bart and Auggie were friends for most of their lives and got into some trouble along the way. They argued a lot like siblings, but always made up. I don't know that they ever came to blows."

Suddenly, a memory shot through me, and I took a deep breath. "Sam, I told you that Bart had anger problems, and I just recalled that he once had a serious fight with an employer of his, about ten or twelve years ago. He was selling something, I'm not sure what, but it was on commission. The guy was cheating Bart out of some money, fudging the books I guess, and they went at it. Bart beat the guy pretty good, and did some short jail time for it."

Sam stiffened as he looked at me. *Maybe I shouldn't have told him.*

"Ooh, that's not good. That means he has an arrest record. Probably won't help him getting bail. Be sure to tell Harry about this. Was he ever arrested for anything else?"

"No, never, just speeding tickets."

Sam scribbled some notes and looked at me. "We know he put the money up front for buying the house and held the majority share of the business. That's what they were arguing about. Money's a recurring theme in Bart's troubles. What else?"

"Teresa," I said. "Bart's taken a strong liking to her, he might even love her. We can't say the same for Auggie. He was cool to her, at best."

Sam wrote some more before looking up from his pad. "We have two points of conflict between Bart and Auggie: money and Teresa. Let's talk about her. She showed up, unannounced, and claims to be a descendent of Ocean Born Mary. Her story checks out, and she gets a job in the business. She wants to do more than sell trinkets at the house; and Bart wants her to do tours, be more high profile, maybe use her for publicity. Auggie is reluctant about it, but starts to see her potential value."

"And don't forget about her meeting with Auggie and Monty that Bart wasn't invited to. He might have been jealous and/or suspicious that Auggie was trying to steal her away." I sipped my coffee.

"That just points back to these conflict points, love and money. Love often involves jealousy."

Sam tapped his pen on the pad a few times, and his eyes went to the ceiling, as if he was searching for information. "Those are our principal players: Bart and Teresa, and they were both at the séance. That leaves Lucy and Monty."

"Lucy was always unlikeable to me," I responded. "But I guess Bart thought she was okay. She didn't seem to stop her son from being friends with him."

"You said something about her name appearing in the newspapers now and then. What was that about?"

"As I recall, she was arrested once for running some kind of a gambling thing, along with a brothel in Manchester. But I think she beat both of those raps somehow."

Sam jotted some more notes. "So, she was never involved in anything violent that you know of?"

"No. I can't imagine the old bat playing tough, but you never know. It doesn't take much to pull a trigger."

Sam sat up straight. "Hold on, Martha. We've almost forgotten about the gun. Where did that come from? I never noticed Auggie carrying one, but that doesn't mean he didn't keep one in the house. Does Bart own one?"

"No, I don't think so, but he might. My guess is it belonged to Auggie. You better check with Chief Powers about that. I'm sure he's checked the registration on it."

"Good idea. I'll call on him today. I sure hope it doesn't belong to Bart."

My mouth kept drying up on me, no matter how much coffee I sipped. If Bart owned the gun that killed Auggie, he was done for.

"Let's look at Monty," said Sam.

"Ugh, just a conceited old stick in the mud. I might have gotten to know him better awhile ago, but he was more interested in himself. What a big drip."

Sam grinned. "You know, one thing I noticed about him was his change in attitude about the business. At first, he seemed very skeptical. He was quick to brush off the idea, don't you think?"

"Sure, but so was I. Anybody would be. Everybody knows that Allan Royston cooked up a big fraud, the legend and all that. I can't fault Monty for that."

"Of course, but he sure changed his tune when Teresa showed up. He fancies himself as a historian. I wonder how well he checked her story out. You think he took a shine to her, too?"

It never occurred to me that Monty could have an interest in Teresa, but she was a charmer. "I don't know, Sam. Could be. What difference would that make? Both of them were long gone after the séance rehearsal."

"True, but I'm just trying to cover all the bases. Teresa acted humble, but she managed to work her way into the business. She said she only wanted a job, but she got that and more. She wasn't only going to sell junk in the gift shop. She was going to be used in publicity and probably conduct tours at the house. Her profile was on the rise."

I grabbed another piece from my donut and popped it into my mouth. "What are you getting at?"

"She's looking pivotal to me. Bart had the hots for her, but Auggie didn't. If Monty was interested in her too, then both he and Auggie might have had conflicts with Bart about her."

"I can accept that, Sam, but I still say, so what? The only ones in the house were Bart, Auggie and Lucy. The rest of us had all left."

Sam rested his face in one hand, his elbow on the table. His words came out slowly, his eyes boring deep into mine. "What if one of them came back?" He waited for my response.

I sipped more coffee, giving me time to collect my thoughts. "That's an interesting idea I never considered. Hey, Bart told Harry that he went to see her that night, but she wasn't home. Or at least she didn't answer the door."

Sam nodded.

"So we can't account for her whereabouts at the time of the killing. Do you think the ghost floated back into the house and took care of Auggie?"

"Calm down, girl," Sam replied. "I'm just trying to look at possibilities. I suspect we'll hear from her soon, and we can ask her where she was. As for Monty, we'll have to check with him, too. I wonder if he's heard about this yet?"

"The Concord and Manchester newspapers must have it by now, maybe even local television. I bet everyone in Henniker has heard. We'll have to go into town and get a paper, since I'm not a subscriber. We can check the TV news at noon."

It wasn't the kind of publicity that Bart had in mind for the business, but it sure would stir up interest in the legend of Ocean Born Mary, adding a new twist to the whole thing.

Sam pushed away from the table and stood up, still working on his donut. "I'll get the newspapers, both of them. You stay here and take it easy."

"I promise, big boy. Say, would you check my mailbox on the way out? I don't recall getting that stuff yesterday. Maybe there's some good news in there. Wouldn't that be a pleasant surprise, like winning that sweepstakes they advertise on TV? Yeah, some good news would be nice."

Chapter Twenty-Three
September 19, 1975. Henniker, New Hampshire

Martha's request to get her mail triggered Sam's memory, reminding him to swing by his apartment and get his own. When he got it, there was the usual assortment of junk mail and a utility bill, but there was also a stunner.

He knew immediately upon looking at the envelope that it was from Eli—his old friend, and the chief Nazi hunter who had solicited his aid in capturing Augusto Rauf, also known as Arthur Vasile. Sam carried the cluster of envelopes into his apartment. He hurried to the kitchen, where he dropped the collection onto the small table. He flopped into a chair while fingering the letter from Eli, tearing it open. Disappointed that it was only one page, Sam grew bug-eyed at the opening words. Eli had heard from Carol.

His words were somehow both reassuring and troublesome.

Dear Sam,

I received a call from Carol Vasile two days ago. She wouldn't tell me where she was and made me promise not to try to find her, saying that she hasn't made a permanent residence yet. She is okay and thanked me and you for saving her life, even though it was the most frightening experience she could imagine and she still has nightmares about it. Looking back, she realized that Arthur would have harmed her eventually, considering his evil plans for resurrecting Nazism in this country. She admits to having thought of you and what a terrible thing it must have been for you, too, to find this man who was Dr. Mengle's assistant at Auschwitz. For a while, she could only feel sorry for herself, but now understands that you were in emotional pain as well. She said you showed great courage in confronting the situation. She wishes you the best and hopes you will forget that you ever knew her, for it can only bring you both more hurt. That's all she said.

I, too, wish you well, Sam, and regret that I haven't contacted you until now. I am doing fine and have a young woman in my life. Perhaps you will be getting a wedding invitation in the not-too-distant future. I'll tell you more about her later. Take care.

Your friend always,
Eli.

Sam lowered the letter onto the table and rested his elbows beside it, rubbing his forehead. *Where can she be? Why wouldn't she contact me directly? It sounds like she's still suffering.*

Sam realized that he still loved her. Despite his growing affection for Martha, he missed her very much. He pulled out his wallet and fished for the small paper with Eli's phone number, the special one his friend had told him he could call at any time. Staring at it for a moment, his eyes went to the phone across the room. He twisted in his chair, as if he were about to make a move, but something told him not to call. He was frozen in place, not sure what action to take. After a painful moment, he made a decision.

Stuffing the paper back into his wallet released him from the freeze. He gently folded the letter and slid it into the envelope, leaving it on the table as he rose and left his apartment. He needed to stay focused on his task of getting the newspapers and finding the accounts of Auggie's murder. Martha had told him she needed his steady strength, so he had to give her his best effort.

Minutes later, he pulled up to the Henniker Pharmacy and purchased the two newspapers he needed. Sam got the answer to his question immediately; they each had a story about the murder and Bart's arrest. He folded the papers and tucked them under his arm, hurrying out of the store, grateful that the clerk didn't know him.

Chapter Twenty-Four
September 19, 1975, Henniker, New Hampshire

There's something strange about getting your daily mail. It's the most routine thing in the world, and we know that it's usually a bunch of worthless paper destined for the dump, yet we all feel a twinge of excitement when we get it. There's always hope that something interesting will be in the pile of junk. Today was no different, but my usual faint ray of mail hope turned sour. When Sam got back to my apartment, he entered without speaking, glancing at me while I sat on the living room sofa cradling a coffee cup. I could see he was out of sorts.

He dropped the mail beside me on the sofa and went to the kitchen, holding the newspapers under his arm. I figured he was getting coffee and would join me. I was right about the coffee.

"You coming out here, Sam?" I called to him as I flipped through my mail. No answer.

What could possibly have happened in the short time he was gone?

Still holding my cup, I eased myself up off the sofa and joined Sam in the kitchen. He was reading a newspaper that was spread out in front of him. I slid the other one along the table as I moved to the chair opposite him and brought it to a stop in front of me. I examined it to see if there was some horrible twist to the story about Auggie's murder dominating the front page.

"Well, the word is definitely out. There's been a murder in Henniker, and the Ocean Born Mary house is closed." I scanned the story, but found nothing that I didn't already know. "What about yours? Any sensational investigative gems?"

Sam was motionless. That was all I could take.

"Okay, pal, what gives? You went out of here like Detective Joe Friday on a mission, and you came back looking like somebody shot your dog. That would be awful, but you don't own a dog. So what the f—?"

Boy, was I slow on the uptake. There was only one thing that could have taken the wind out of his sails like this. I swallowed hard before asking the question. "You've heard from her, haven't you?"

At first, he just shook his head. When he stopped, his eyes blinked at me once, then stared into mine. "No. Actually, I heard from Eli. She called him."

He quickly explained. The pain on his face was plain to see. *Oh shit. My Superman just swallowed kryptonite. Not now, please, not now. This is a hell of a time for him to be doting over Carol. I need you at full strength, Sam.*

I needed to be strong, too. I needed his help, and he needed mine. *We've got to be that old team again. The cost is too high not to be.*

"I know you still love her, Sam. I've always known it. Believe me, I don't expect that to change, and I'm not going to give you that speech about letting go, because I know you won't. But I am going to ask you to push her memory aside for a while. You've lost your love, but I'm about to lose my brother because of a murder I'm sure he didn't commit."

Something clicked in him. I could see it, a fast flinch, like he had just been pricked with a needle. His eyes found me again. "I'm sorry. I fell into selfish mode, thinking only of my loss. She's been gone for over a year, and she was never in love with me. I was on a one-way street. You're right. Bart is in serious trouble. You've already lost a brother in the war. You can't lose another one. Forgive me, but Eli's letter was a shock. I'll get over it. Let me freshen up my coffee, and we'll see what these newspapers have to say."

I accepted his words by showing a tight-lipped grin. Sam was back. I hoped he'd stay a while, a long while. He refilled his cup and returned to the table.

We examined the news stories of the murder and concluded that they were just bland surface reports. But they were enough to inform the community that another murder mystery had hit Henniker, just about a year after the last one. *What is happening to my small town?*

"We can't stay holed up here in my apartment, Sam. We've got to do something. Maybe I should go in to work."

"No, don't do that, not today. We've called in for the day, so we're going to take all of it. But I agree we've got to get moving, so let's go look for Teresa."

Those words brought a smile to my face, and I jumped out of my chair. In a minute we were in my car, but this time I drove.

We didn't speak during the short drive. It was as if we had both found a determination that had gone astray for a brief time. My foot got heavy on the gas pedal.

Once at Teresa's apartment, I knocked, but got no response. We looked at each other before Sam tried his knuckles on the door. Again, no response.

I squinted at Sam. "You think she left town?"

"Could be, but it doesn't make sense. She was headed home right after the séance."

"Yeah, but Bart went looking for her later that night, and she wasn't around. Maybe she never went home." My jaw dropped as I looked hard at Sam. "Maybe she never made it home. Maybe something happened to her, too."

For a moment Sam looked like he shared that concern, but it passed. "This isn't a Bogart movie. There aren't any usual suspects. Everybody's been accounted for."

"Not everybody." Our eyes met, and we spoke in unison, "Monty."

We dashed back to my car and sped off to the Henniker Historical Society.

"They keep limited hours, don't they?" asked Sam.

"Yes, but I think this is open time for them. I hope."

We arrived at the old wooden church building that housed the HHS in its basement and hurried to the door. I grabbed the knob and expected a fight from the lock, but it was open.

The Society had a small main room that we entered. Historical items: documents, photos, books and brochures adorned the walls and tables. Nobody was around so, with Sam leading, we headed for an adjoining room that had a sign over the door: Dr. M. Phillips. Before we got there, Sam stopped at a display table. He shot a look at me and pointed to an old kitchen knife in the display. "Just like the one in the house," he whispered.

"Later, Buster," I replied, waving him onward.

Monty was seated at his desk studying a newspaper. His face told me that he was reading about Auggie, and he didn't look up at first.

"Good morning, Monty. Got a minute?"

He came out of his trance when I spoke. His eyes were glazed.

"Oh, good morning, Martha and Sam. I was just reading about this terrible thing. What a shock. I'm surprised you're not visiting your brother. What are you doing here? What do you want with me?"

Sam stepped in front of me, getting closer to Monty's desk. "We need to talk."

Monty looked confused and worried. "Yes, yes, pull up those chairs. Sorry we don't have a conference room." He pointed to a couple of old wooden chairs against a wall.

Sam and I each grabbed one and set them in front of Monty's desk. I squirmed in my chair, signaling that I was about to speak, but Sam jumped in ahead of me.

"Since you've read that article, you know what happened to Auggie, and that Bart's been arrested. He's being arraigned today, and we won't be able to see him for a few days, maybe a week. We got him a lawyer, and he's spoken with Bart."

"Yes, well I guess he's got to have a lawyer, but who would take the case? Looks like they caught him red handed, so to speak, gun in hand. What can I do?"

"Never mind about the lawyer," I snapped. "What you can do is tell us everything you know."

Monty put on his best indignant face. "What? Look, this article says they caught Bart with the gun in his hands. Are you interrogating me? What gives you the right?"

Sam jumped in. "Look, Monty, we're trying to stay ahead of the police. They think they've got their man, so they haven't come around to us, but they will. You can be sure of that. We'll probably all be questioned soon, maybe today. They know who the players were at the séance and will have to question us all."

Monty's hands were together on his desk, thumbs rubbing. "Yes, I suppose that makes sense. Does that include Willa, the medium?"

"I don't see why not," said Sam.

"How will they find her? Has Bart told them about her and everybody at the séance?"

"No, he has the right to remain silent, remember? His lawyer told him to keep quiet. But Lucy has probably given them the news about the séance, and everything else she knows about that night, as long as she was awake." I shot my mouth off. Sam's head snapped toward me, and he fired me a piercing glare. I got the message and shut up.

Sam continued, "Lucy can tell them about Willa and surely has her phone number somewhere. Do you know anything about her?"

"No, last night was the first I ever heard of her. I don't know how Bart or Auggie came to hire her. I don't know why you think I have anything to offer that you don't already know. You were there, too."

"You believe the séance was legit. Am I wrong?"

"No Sam, you're not wrong. But when you say *legit,* let me clarify. I didn't observe anything that was an obvious trick. There were no strings, wires, hidden speakers or anything like that. As far as Teresa's performance, I believe she truly was experiencing something, but I don't know what. She had never met the medium, as far as I know. They couldn't have had time to rehearse anything. In fact, last night *was* the rehearsal, wasn't it? It was a very good show, but Teresa will have to explain things for herself."

"Okay," said Sam. "What about her story, you know, about her lineage to Ocean Born Mary? You checked her out, correct?"

Monty squirmed. "Well, I looked at her papers—the receipts from that school—and they looked authentic enough."

"You mean you never called anybody? You said you had some friends you could talk to about her. I gather that didn't happen."

"What was I going to do, tell them that the ghost of Ocean Born Mary had just come to town? I believed those receipts told it all and saw no need to do anything else."

Sam and I exchanged looks as if to say *what's next?* Sam leaned forward in his chair.

"Like I said, we're trying to stay ahead of the police. Maybe we can help each other."

Monty relaxed a little after those words. He went from rubbing his thumbs to tapping his fingertips together. "Yes, perhaps you're right. Let's try to help each other. But wait a minute. You don't think the police suspect any of us as accomplices, do you? I mean, they caught Bart right there with a gun. They were the only ones there, I assume."

"The police won't assume anything." Monty looked nervous again after Sam's remark. He was on an emotional rollercoaster. Sam tried a softer tone. "Monty, have you heard from Teresa?"

"No, I haven't. So, you haven't talked to her yet. Maybe we should go over to her place."

"We already did, and she wasn't home." Sam looked straight at Monty, avoiding my stare. I waited for Sam to explain that Bart had gone after her late last night, but I realized he didn't want to reveal anything we had learned from Harry.

Sam is better than me at thinking on his feet, even if he is sitting down.

"Maybe we should try again?"

"You can call her if you want, Monty, but I don't think there'd be anything to gain if a party of three showed up at her door. Martha and I will keep trying to find her. She might be trying to find us, for that matter. She had shown an interest in Bart, so I'm sure she's concerned. If the police come to talk to you, cooperate truthfully. We'll be in touch."

We said farewell to Monty and hustled out of the place. Something about his look had bothered me. Sam stayed behind me as we moved, and I turned to look at him, anxious to ask him if he had seen what I saw. He wouldn't let me stop, however, and kept nudging me along. I tried again, another look, another nudge.

I waited until we were in the car before speaking. "Sam, there was something strange about Monty through that whole thing. Did you notice?"

"I only noticed that he never did a thorough check on Teresa's story. Although they could have been forged, those receipts she showed us were very convincing. They would have to have been done professionally to look that good, and she doesn't seem to have that kind of operation going for her."

"Well, I thought his eyes were kind of moist when we arrived, like he'd been crying. You didn't notice?"

"No, can't say that I did. Maybe it was the dingy air in that office."

I took in a breath and eased it out as I started the car. "Maybe, maybe. What do we do now?"

"I'd like to do what Monty should have done. Let's do some real checking on her story."

"Fine, but how?"

"We've got the whole day. Let's go down to Massachusetts and visit that school. What was it, Fitzgerald Hall?"

"That's in Wellesley. I know how to get there, but I've never seen the school. I'm sure we can find it, 'cause I'm not afraid to ask for directions."

Sam chuckled. "How long do you think it will take us?"

"About an hour and twenty, maybe thirty. We can make a food stop along the way. No problem." I looked at my gas gauge. It was half full. "I'd better top it off before we go."

Chapter Twenty-Five
September 19, 1975, Wellesley, Massachusetts

By the time we got to Wellesley, my stomach was growling like a wolf. "Sam, we'd better stop for lunch. I don't want to go talking to people while my stomach is mad at me. Besides, it's about the time when staffers will be having lunch. We might have a better chance of finding a helpful one if we give them a little more time."

"Okay, find us a fast food place so we can slow down."

We drove through a small commercial section and spotted a diner. It was after one o'clock when we finished our meals and motored to Fitzgerald Hall. We stopped at a campus map and directory at the entrance of the school.

"What do you think, the administration building first, Sam?"

He shook his head. "No, I don't think so. Let's try the library. They're used to helping people find things, and they just might have historical records on microfilm there."

Following the campus map, the library was easy to find. If I were making a movie and needed a college library, this place would do the trick. A two-story brownstone, it looked like a place where scholarly work was done. We exited the car and entered the stately building.

There is a stereotypical look assigned to librarians; female, short, dark hair and horn-rimmed glasses. Not the case here. A tall, athletic looking man in his early thirties worked the main desk. I didn't mind.

"Hello. Can I help you?" His voice had an Orson Welles twang to it, much to my delight. His smile was contagious, and I beamed one right back at him.

"I certainly hope so. I'm Martha Sanborn, and this is my colleague, Sam Miller. We work at New Sussex College in New Hampshire."

"Ah," he interrupted. "That would be Henniker, New Hampshire, correct?"

Sam and I gazed at each other, not expecting this recognition. "Nice to know you've heard of it. NSC is very small," I replied.

"Yes," he said, "but the town of Henniker is a bit infamous, what with that terrible news last year about the college president and some Nazi war criminal, and—not to mention—the legend of Ocean Born Mary."

We did the eyeball-to-eyeball look again.

"So you know about that," I said.

"Oh, yes. We have an old book about it in our collection. I think it was donated."

"Well, you're going to be surprised to find out that we're here because of that legend. Say, I didn't catch your name." I had to hear more of that great voice.

"I'm sorry," he said. "I'm Bill Clark."

"You see, Bill, we're doing some research around the legend, and we have reason to believe that a relative of Ocean Born Mary's attended this school in 1835. We're trying to determine if that's true."

"That should be easy enough," said Bill. "We have a full directory of everyone who has ever attended Fitzgerald Hall. It's all on microfiche. I'll be happy to show you."

Handsome Bill led us to a section devoted to school history, and found a drawer of student records. "Are you familiar with how to use a microfiche reader?"

"Yes, indeed, Mr. Bill. We also work in a library."

"Fine. What year were you looking for?"

"1835," said Sam.

Bill ran his fingertip through the drawer of microfiche and retrieved one for me. "Here it is. They're all numbered, so if this one doesn't have what you're looking for, just go up the numbers on the fiche. There's a reader against that wall. I'll let you have at it. Good luck."

Sam took a seat at that ugly looking thing called a microfiche reader, which seemed out of place in a building devoted to books. He placed the fiche in the holder and found the power switch. He twisted the crank that moved the fiche so he could scroll to the section he needed, and I watched for it on the large viewing screen, my hands resting on his shoulders.

"Bingo! There she is: Sarah Winslow, Londonderry, New Hampshire." Sam twisted in his chair and gave me a wink.

"Wow, that was quick," I said. "We spent over two hours getting here, and we're done in five minutes. Don't you love this new technology?" I changed my mind about those clumsy-looking machines.

"We can thank our friend Bill for being so cooperative and eager to help. Embrace the power of the librarian, Martha."

"What about Teresa? I guess this proves she's on the level. Nobody in Londonderry could know about Sarah Winslow except her direct family. She was sent away to this boarding school as a young girl. She was well hidden. But while we're here, should we try to find the record of payments, the original bills sent to Sarah's mother?" Something kept me from placing full trust in Teresa.

Sam looked at me with a raised eyebrow. "I guess it won't hurt to try, since we're here. Let's find the Business Office, but I doubt they'll have anything."

Sam led the way, and soon we were talking to a clerk. She stifled a laugh when we told her what we wanted and informed us that they didn't keep records that far back. *Okay, no harm in trying.*

"Let's head home, my man, while the traffic is still light."

"Do you want me to drive, Martha? I don't mind."

"No, but thanks anyway. I'm okay. Let's go."

Chapter Twenty-Six
Friday, September 24, 1975, Henniker, New Hampshire

Time seemed to crawl like a wounded turtle as I waited to hear from Harry Parsons. It hurt to think of Bart in lock-up, and I yearned to see and speak to him. Finally, a week later, I got the call while at work on Friday afternoon. I was cleared to visit my brother. I raced to Sam's office.

"I heard from Harry, and I can visit Bart. I'm going right after work."

"We're going, my lady. Of course, I'll join you. You're so hyped up, I'm afraid you might crash into a tree. I'll drive."

Sam was being a good protector again, and it sent warmth through me. *Hurry up, five o'clock.*

We dropped my car off at my apartment, where I ran inside to grab some snack food, before jumping into Sam's vehicle.

"I can't wait to see him. He must be so depressed."

"Think positive, hon. This will be the best day he's had in awhile. I sure hope we see somebody else soon, too."

I knew who Sam was talking about. There still was no sign of Teresa. That couldn't be good.

It felt like it took much longer to drive to the fairly new county jail then it actually did. It was a fresh-looking, brick building on the outside, but inside the halls were lined with cinder block, typical early-American-penitentiary décor. After being escorted to a large room for visitations, we were seated at a cubicle with Plexiglas shielding us from contact with prisoners. A phone handset was available on both sides, necessary since the glass partition went up to the ceiling.

I bit my lip when I saw Bart emerge through a door, being escorted by a guard. He was cuffed, with a chain that led to ankle clasps, and wearing a jumpsuit. I've never seen him look so downtrodden. He seemed to show a microscopic smile when he looked at me. It got bigger as they got closer. I held back tears as he was seated across from us, and I hugged the phone.

"Oh, Bart. It's so good to finally see you. I can't believe this is happening."

"Me neither, Mart. This is a miserable place. I hope you can get me out."

Sam said, "We've only got a few minutes, Bart, so we have to get to business. Sorry."

Sam should have been a lawyer.

"First," Sam continued. "Tell me, straight to my face, Bart—did you kill Auggie?"

It startled me that Sam would ask that question, but I saw him stare deep into my brother's eyes, and I understood. Bart could lie to me and be convincing under the circumstances, but he could not pull one over Sam. I guess he learned a lot about lying at Auschwitz.

"Of course not. That's the truth."

They stared silently for a moment before Sam nodded. "I believe you, Bart."

Sam turned to me with a look that said he was okay with Bart's answer. He got back to business. *Are you sure you're not a lawyer?*

"We know you've been through this with the police and Harry, but we have to hear it from you. What happened after the séance?"

Bart took a deep breath, the kind that says *oh no, not again.* I could see the pain on his face.

"Okay, everyone but Teresa left. When we had finished our conversation, I offered to take her home, but she declined. She insisted that she was fine and could drive herself, so I reluctantly agreed. Lucy went to bed, but Auggie and I had a drink in the kitchen, and we talked about the evening. We agreed it went well, and he thought that Teresa really sold it, meaning she was faking it. That pissed me off. We kept drinking and talking, and we focused on Teresa's business deal."

"I thought you just hired her as a worker, and that you didn't have to make a special deal with her." My voice went up a notch.

Bart swallowed hard, looking down. "Well, that was what we planned when we first met her, but things changed."

"How so?" asked Sam.

"We met with her a few days before the séance, and she said she wanted a bigger stake in things. She said that she knew what a fraud this legend was and thought it made her family look bad. She said—in a very soft, convincing tone—that she would go public with her story and denounce Royston and all that he had done at the house. She could destroy our business if she wasn't given more. We asked her what she wanted."

Sam looked at me. "I can feel her squeeze play now."

Bart resumed, "She said she wanted a third ownership, insisting that her lineage was true, and that she was our best bet for getting people to believe in the legend. But Auggie and I could not bring ourselves to hand over a third of the equity in the business and property. We convinced her that the real estate belonged to us, whether the legend died or not. It was not part of the deal. I guess we got her on that, so she agreed to our offer."

"Which was what?" I didn't like any of this.

"We offered her a one-third partnership to cover only revenue received from all cash sales. You know, tours, merchandise, anything that was in the cash flow. That would be far better than a simple wage. She agreed."

Sam looked at me. "Maybe she did fake it at the séance, as a way of bolstering her position. If she did it at a public séance and was convincing, it would help in showing that she was the real deal, a descendent of Mary's, and able to be in touch with the ghost. Maybe Auggie was right."

Bart looked at Sam as if somebody had shot his puppy. "I don't believe that. Teresa and I had begun to get close. When she sprang this deal on us, it hurt, but I came around to the idea that it was best for the business, and she was just looking out for herself. After all, the Wallace family was wealthy, but her side got nothing because of Robert's illicit affair with Sarah. I couldn't blame her."

Sam leaned into the phone. "But Auggie could."

"Yes, he hated the idea all along. That became quite evident after more drinks. We started yelling at each other."

Bart looked at me as if he were about to speak, his mouth open. But he shut his jaw and diverted his gaze.

"What is it, Bart? Is there something else?"

"Yes, I almost forgot. Teresa wanted to know what would happen if either of us were incapacitated in some way, or even died. She insisted on knowing this. I explained that we had a clause in our incorporation that the assets of the business would fall to the surviving partner or partners. Auggie reminded her that it would not include the real estate in her case, and we would modify the clause as such."

I looked at Sam. "She would still take an increased share of the business if one of you died or became unable to work. That might not be enough to be a motive for murder, but she certainly wanted a bigger share."

Sam scratched his chin like a man in deep thought. "You say that the two of you were getting close. Do you mean that in a romantic sense?"

"Yes, I guess you could say that. I was falling in love with her."

Sam swung his head my way and back at Bart. "Do you think it could lead to marriage?"

That question hit me like a sucker punch.

Bart took a deep breath before answering. "I suppose I had the idea of a long-term thing with her, but I never said that. I've never been interested in marriage before, but Teresa is different from any woman I've ever known."

Sam continued. "If you and Teresa were married and Auggie died, you would be the sole owner of the property, and she would be your wife. I'm sure she'd want to be her husband's beneficiary. Then she'd share everything with you."

Bart's face flushed. "You don't think she could have killed Auggie, do you? It doesn't make sense. After all, we're not married. We're not even engaged. Wouldn't it make more sense for her if she were already married to me?"

I grabbed Sam's arm. "Maybe not," I said. "Maybe she was taking it one step at a time. She might think she could manipulate you into a marriage if you were alone in running the business and needed her help and comfort."

"But Mart, if I go to prison for murder, she has no claim on the property."

"True, but maybe she didn't count on you being arrested. Sometimes plans go wrong."

Bart shook his head. "I don't think there was a plan. I can't believe it. Teresa is smart, and I don't blame her for trying to look out for herself. I can't accept that she is a killer."

"I don't like to accuse her," I said, "and I'm not. But we have to be open to all possibilities, and the fact that she has disappeared is very suspicious. We have to find her soon."

Sam looked from me to Bart, as if assessing our points of view.

"Bart, you said you and Auggie were yelling at each other. Did you fight, physically?"

"No, Sam. I swear I never touched him. After a while, he quieted down and actually changed his point of view. He apologized to me, and we hugged and made up, like we usually do. He wanted us to have another drink, but I said no. I was worried about Teresa and went out to find her, to check up. But she wasn't home, so I came right back to the house. Then it all hit the fan."

"Take it slowly. What next, exactly." Sam was cool, but I was grinding my teeth.

"I drove around back of the house and went in through the kitchen. I found Auggie on the floor, clutching his gut. There was a pool of blood. It was awful. I went up to him and found a gun lying beside him. I don't know why I did it, but I picked up the gun to look at it. That was stupid, I know. Anyway, I heard Auggie groan and was relieved that he was alive. I asked him who did it, but he couldn't talk. His eyes caught mine, and he tried to say something, but just gurgled. I couldn't understand him. Then he fell back, flat on the floor. I rushed to the kitchen phone, still holding the gun, and called for an ambulance, then went back to Auggie."

Sam stirred in his seat. "Was he still alive?"

"I'm not sure. Just then, Lucy appeared in the kitchen from the hallway. She saw me with Auggie, holding the gun. She screamed like holy hell, 'You killed my son, you killed my son,' and ran back upstairs. I could hear her door slam shut, and I guess she locked herself in. She probably thought I was going to kill her, but I stayed with Auggie, trying to stop the bleeding. It was no use. I must have tried for several minutes, pressing my hands against the wound. In a short while, the cops showed up. They had guns drawn, aimed at me. I realized they thought I was the killer. Soon after that, the ambulance showed up at the back of the house. I had told them to do that. The EMTs came in and looked at Auggie, checking for life, but they said he was dead."

Bart rubbed his hands against his face.

"Keep going," said Sam.

"It got really bad," said Bart. "Lucy came back into the kitchen. I guess hearing the police arrive made her feel safe. She said she had called the police from her room after finding me over her son with a gun in my hand. She was screaming that she'd heard me and Auggie shouting at each other over the business and the money, but then everything went quiet for a while. She was scared and didn't dare leave her room, claiming that there was more arguing and a gunshot, maybe two. She thought she heard someone moving around in the kitchen, and there was a car that pulled up a few minutes later. I guess that was mine. She finally worked up the courage to come downstairs and saw me with the gun. Then she ran back upstairs, locked herself in her room and called the police. They arrested me, and I guess you know the rest."

Sam looked puzzled. "So she heard movement in the kitchen before she heard your car arrive?"

"I think that's what she said. She was hysterical at that point, so her memory might be untrustworthy." Bart shook his head, like a man in despair.

The story left me stunned. It was like something from a TV show, but worse. This had actually happened. I believed every word Bart said. *We have to save him, but how?*

Chapter Twenty-Seven
Saturday, September 27, 1975, Henniker, New Hampshire

Sam and I decided to go out for breakfast.

We were sitting in a booth at The Nook when Chief Cal Powers walked in and spotted us. We were halfway through our eggs and pancakes when Sam, who was facing in that direction, waved him over. "Hi, Cal, won't you join us?"

"Don't mind if I do. I'm just taking a coffee break, so I can't stay long. Hi, Martha." He slid in beside me. *He's pretty nimble for a big guy.*

"I'm sure sorry about your brother's situation, Martha. I see you've got Harry Parsons handling his case. He's a good man and should do a fine job. I'm surprised you're not at the jail this morning."

I looked at the chief for a moment. He had earned my respect last year when Sam and I were nearly run off the road and into the river. "Thanks, Chief," I said. "I know Bart is innocent. We've just got to prove it. Easier said than done, huh?"

A waitress took Cal's order.

"I have to admit that it doesn't look good, what with him being found with the gun in his hand while standing over the victim. Not good at all."

"But Cal, Bart didn't have any reason to kill Auggie," I insisted. "Somebody else was in the house while Bart was out looking for Teresa Thurgood. Bart found Auggie on the floor in the kitchen after he was shot."

The waitress delivered Cal's coffee, and he took a swallow before replying. "I know that's his story, but he's going to need proof."

"But he still had no reason for killing his partner and friend. That doesn't make sense."

"Look, Martha, it could have been done in the heat of the moment." Cal gazed at me and Sam. "Lucy said they were arguing loudly, a fight over the business. Maybe Auggie showed the gun, and they struggled. Such things happen."

Sam's eye's opened wide. "The gun, Cal. Were you able to trace it?"

"Sure enough. It was Auggie Raymond's."

"Well, that's a minor relief," I said. "That at least argues against premeditation, doesn't it?"

"Perhaps," said Cal. "It gives your lawyer a better chance of getting the murder charge reduced."

I turned slightly toward Cal. "We think someone else had a motive for killing Auggie." I went on to explain Teresa's involvement, and how she wrangled a deal out of my brother and his partner.

"That's all very interesting, but it's pure conjecture. If true, I'd have to say she's a pretty smart cookie, setting this plot up in stages until she's left with the business and property. That property is probably worth around $100 thousand, and it appears they're bringing in some decent money with the legend and all the stuff associated with it."

Sam tilted his head to one side, as if he were shaking loose an idea. "There may be more than just the monetary value. Her side of the family was always left out in the cold. Maybe she wants the satisfaction of beating the Wallace clan."

"You mean getting the last laugh?" Cal pondered the idea. "Could be. I'll relay this to the State Police, but they feel their investigation is closed, and they've got their man. You're going to have to come up with some pretty convincing evidence to make them change their minds. So far, the evidence all points to Bart. Unless directed otherwise, I have no authority to investigate further, but I know how you two like to get to the bottom of things. There's no reason why you can't keep asking questions, as long as you're not breaking any laws."

"Wait a minute," I blurted out. "How can they close the case without finding Teresa and questioning her?"

"Find Teresa?" Cal showed a quizzed look. "Heck, she came in a couple of days ago and spoke to me. The Staties came to my office and took her statement. She was quite upset about the murder and wanted to see Bart, but I told her she would have to wait."

Sam and I were dumbfounded. "Chief, we've been trying to find her ever since the incident."

Cal sipped more coffee. "All I can tell you is that she said she left the séance and decided to drive to Londonderry to stay with relatives. She didn't hear about the murder until a few days ago. That's when she drove back to Henniker and came to me."

"That would explain why Bart couldn't find her that night, and why we haven't seen her either." That idea had escaped us.

"Why don't you go see her at the house?" Cal shot a look at each of us. "She called in this morning and asked when she could resume the business. I told her she could do that anytime, now that Bart has been arraigned and the State Police have finished checking out the place. We're also letting Lucy move back in. We've put her up at a motel in Hillsboro for the time being. They're probably both back there now. Why don't you go talk to her?"

"You're damned right we will," I said. "Please excuse us, Chief."

Cal eased his big frame out of the booth to let me exit. Sam dropped some cash on the table, and we hustled out to the car. I was pissed off that we had missed her for several days, but at the same time I was relieved that she was apparently back in town.

When we arrived at the house, it looked peaceful, a stark contrast to all of the recent police attention that had kept us away since the séance.

"It seems strange to see the place so vacant, Sam. There are no tourists or gawkers around. They must have been scared off by the murder."

Sam smirked. "People back away from death, for many reasons. But it can change quickly. The same death can become a magnet for curiosity hounds. They'll be back."

I hadn't thought of it that way. A man like Allan Royston might use Auggie's death as another part of the legend. He might even create another ghost to haunt the house. Auggie might even do the same thing, if he wasn't the dead man.

We entered through the front door, which was unlocked. There was a shuffling noise from the gift shop, and a voice called out.

"Martha, Sam, hello! I'm so glad to see you." Teresa was wearing a flowing blue dress over a white silk blouse, the kind of look she sported when working. We exchanged hugs, which I could have done without.

"Are you here alone? We spoke to Chief Powers, and he said Lucy was being brought back, too." I gazed around but saw no one else.

"No, I'm not alone. Lucy is here, too. She saw me when I arrived, but didn't say anything and went up to her room. She hasn't made a peep since."

"You're not open for business, are you? If not, you might want to lock the front door, just in case curious people show up."

Sam looked at me and pointed a finger in the air. "I'll get it," he said.

Teresa called to him as he moved away. "Thank you, Sam. I hadn't thought of that. No, I'm not ready for business yet. I'll need to get some help together first. Right now

I'm just cleaning up a bit and checking the inventory." She gazed around the room with a lost look, as if she didn't know where to begin. "Have you seen Bart yet? I hope I can see him soon."

"Yes, we've talked to him, and I got him a lawyer." I needed to switch the focus of the conversation. "Teresa, let's go sit in the dining room. We need to talk."

Her face is blank. Maybe her mind is, too.

Teresa slid into a chair at one end of the table, while Sam and I sat next to each other, me closest to her. I wanted to know about the statement she had given to the police. She told us about leaving the séance and going to Londonderry.

"So you didn't know that Bart came looking for you at your apartment right after the séance?"

"No, of course not."

"Bart was very worried about you. Why did you go to Londonderry?"

"After the séance, I felt strange. I guess I needed to be close to family. I still have cousins there." She didn't make eye contact with me while talking, her gaze floating about the room.

"When did you learn of the murder? Why didn't you come right back?"

"I came back as soon as I heard about it, but that was two days ago. I don't read newspapers much and don't watch television, my cousins and I are alike on that, but one of them finally heard about it and told me. That's when I came back and went to see the police. The chief told me I could return to the house, and I could try to see Bart this afternoon. I'm sure he'll want me to get the business going again, but I need to assemble some help."

"I can understand you going to be with relatives, but by disappearing, you almost got into real trouble." As soon as I finished speaking, I felt Sam's foot tap mine. I got the message.

"What do you mean?" Teresa began to show some color in her cheeks, and her voice had an edge to it.

Sam jumped in. "The police needed to speak to all of us from the séance, that's all. Now they have your statement, and you're fine."

"Oh, yes, they have it." She lost the edge in her voice.

I paused before speaking, not wanting to anger Sam's foot again. "Before you left the séance, did you get a chance to speak with Auggie?"

"As a matter of fact, I did. I went into the kitchen to get some water. Bart offered to get a glass for me, but I said I was feeling okay and could do it myself. Bart went over to Monty, and I assumed Auggie joined him. But as I was at the sink running the water, he appeared beside me, and he put his hand on my shoulder. He spoke in a quiet voice about how much he liked the séance, and how well I had done. He said he had changed his mind, that he didn't think I was a money grabber, and that I was going to be a real asset to the business."

"How did you feel about that?" I knew how Auggie could change to match the circumstances.

"Well, when he said it, I felt good that he was not my opponent after all. But then he started rubbing my back, running his hand down, reaching just below my waist. I was surprised by his actions and turned away, saying I wanted to leave. He stopped touching me and followed me out of the kitchen into the dining room. Bart was with Monty, but he turned in time to see me and Auggie come into the room. I guess we looked like we were together, and Bart didn't look happy. But I went to him and gave him a hug, saying I was feeling well and was going to leave. He walked me out to my car and kissed me goodnight before I drove away."

"Wow," I said. "Auggie was actually coming on to you? But Bart didn't see that, right?"

"Right, he just saw us walking out of the kitchen together. By the look on his face, he must have thought Auggie was trying something with me."

"That's a surprise," I said. "I always thought Auggie swung from the other side. I mean, according to Bart, he occasionally saw a hooker or got his rocks off with a girl from one of his schemes, but I always had the impression—well, you know."

Teresa peered at me. "He was definitely trying to make a move on me, the way he touched me, and the way he spoke. I wasn't born yesterday."

"This doesn't help Bart," said Sam. "It might introduce jealousy as another motive for him to kill Auggie. Was that in your statement to the police?"

"No, I didn't mention that. In fact, I had forgotten about it until just now."

Sam nodded. "Good, let's leave that one alone. It may be nothing, after all, so let's not add fuel to the fire. So, what else did you tell the police?"

"That's it. Bart walked me out, and I drove away, deciding to go to Londonderry."

"Have you spoken to anyone else since you got back?" I asked.

"No, I haven't."

"What about Monty?" asked Sam.

She shook her head.

Teresa was either being sincere, or she was a great actress. I felt sorry for her. I wanted to see how she acted in front of Bart. "We're going to the jail after lunch, Teresa, why don't you ride with us?"

Her face brightened. "Oh, that would be great. Thank you, so much."

"Just wait for us here. Sam and I will be back, and we'll all go together."

It was too early for lunch, but I wanted some time alone with Sam so we could compare thoughts about Teresa and her story. We went back to my place. Sam eased himself onto the sofa, and I snuggled up beside him.

"What do you think of her, old boy? Does her account of things add up for you?"

"I'm not sure," said Sam. "Her going to Londonderry lends some credibility to her performance at the séance. She might have just been confused or overwhelmed by the medium, or maybe she really thought she was feeling the presence of Mary's ghost. I think that happens to people at séances, you know, they want so badly to believe that they hyperventilate and faint. That might have compelled her to tell her relatives, so off to Londonderry she goes. Say, were you serious about thinking Auggie was gay?"

"Not really. It's just the impression I've always had of him. Once Bart said that Auggie could get a little too friendly after drinking, that he even gave Bart a smooch on the cheek a couple of times, or the occasional pat on the ass. Bart never thought much of it, but just when he was getting convinced his old friend was gay, he'd see Auggie make it with a girl at a party or something. I guess Bart never worried about it, so neither should I."

"Fair enough," said Sam. He put his wonderful hands on me, and I thought he was going to suggest some fun, but he was just clearing me away as he rose up from the sofa. "I think I'll see if I can reach Harry Parsons before we go to see Bart. I want to make sure he knows that Teresa is back in town."

"Okay, his card is pinned next to the phone."

I rummaged through a small pile of magazines on an end table beside the sofa, while Sam dialed. As I spread them out, I spotted a recent copy of *Yankee* magazine about a third of the way down the pile, and slid it into my hands. *Yankee* often had articles about vintage New England houses and gave a brief history about the ownership. It must have had a story at one time about the Ocean Born Mary house, and I'm sure Bart and Auggie had it among their targets for publicity opportunities. I killed some time with the magazine, while Sam talked to Harry.

Momentarily distracted by a story about a novelist on Cape Cod and the old house she lived in, I heard the sound of Sam hanging up the phone. In seconds, he was standing in front of me. "I gave him a quick rundown on Teresa's story and told him she was traveling with us to see Bart. He's going to give us about a half hour with your brother before joining us. He sounded really interested in meeting her."

I nodded as I gazed up at the most important man in my life. Funny how your moods can shift and change. My worries about Bart became subdued, and Sam's presence took hold of me. I put my fingertip on his kneecap and traced a small circle. He got the message and stepped back, waving me toward the stairs. Passing time with a magazine is fine, but passing it in Sam's embrace is far better.

Chapter Twenty-Eight

Sunday, September 28, 1975. Henniker, New Hampshire

The visit with Bart the day before made me feel a lot better. He was so thrilled to see Teresa. Somehow, it lifted my spirits as well. I wanted this feeling to last as long as possible.

My phone rang shortly after nine o'clock. It caught me by surprise and rekindled my worries. *Who could this be?* Sam was upstairs, and Bart couldn't be calling me. Maybe Harry. I inched my way to the kitchen wall phone and lifted the receiver to my ear. "Hello."

"Hello, Martha. It's Monty. I'm so glad to have reached you."

I wasn't sure if I was happy or sad. "Good morning, Monty. How are you?"

"As a matter of fact, I'm fine. Today should be a good day, and I hope you can share it with me."

"Oh, what's got you in such a good mood?" *I always think he's up to something.*

"I'm sorry to be giving you short notice, but well, I only put this together yesterday. I'm having a small event today at the Historical Society. Nothing major, but I've called a few people, and they're coming over this afternoon. I even posted some signs around town yesterday. It's like a yard sale, of a sort. I'm discounting some items in our shop and offering refreshments, too. Some of the college faculty will be coming, and I hope you can join us. You and Sam. What do you say?"

He sounded really upbeat, but I figured he must be worried about bad attendance, since he had put the event together on short notice. *Why else would he invite me and Sam?* "What time?" I asked.

"It's from one to six. What do you say? So you'll come?"

"Well, I have to check with Sam, but I think we can stop by. You realize that you're competing with football on TV?" I didn't think Monty gave a fig about football, but his intended audience might.

"Oh yes, I know. That's why I'll go up to six o'clock. One to four should be the slow time, then watch out from four to six." Monty blurted a laugh. "I'm just kidding, you know. Like I said, it's not a big deal, but there should be enough people to make it fun. I look forward to seeing you."

"Okay. I'll tell Sam, and we'll swing by, but it will probably be after football. See you later."

I heard Sam's footsteps coming down the stairs, and he met me in the kitchen as I poured myself a cup of coffee.

"Who's calling on a Sunday morning? Everything okay? The coffee smells good. I think I'll join you."

I slipped into a seat at the end of the kitchen table and held back my answer to Sam's question until he parked himself near me. I sipped my coffee and sent him a smile. "That was Monty calling to invite us to a not so big deal at the Historical Society."

"How's that?"

"He was rambling about having something like a yard sale at the Historical Society." I gave Sam the details. "It shouldn't interfere with football watching if we go late."

"Oh, I'm not that concerned about the Patriots game. They're pretty rotten this year, and they're playing Miami, so they'll get clobbered. Why don't we go early and get it over with?"

He's right about the Patriots. I wonder if they'll ever have a decent team. They couldn't even build a stadium with good plumbing. "I'm good with that idea. Let's beat the crowd, all five of them."

Sam smiled in agreement, and I began to spin my wheels, looking at the ceiling. "You know, Monty always struck me as a detailed type of guy, not somebody who did things spur of the moment. And he was very cheerful. I wonder what he's got up his sleeve?"

"I know you don't like the guy, but a yard sale—or whatever it is—seems pretty tame."

"Maybe, but I believe my brother is innocent, and that leaves just three people from the séance who could be the killer: Teresa, Lucy and Monty."

Sam placed his cup down. "Whoa, you're including Lucy? How do you figure?"

"I don't know. I'm just trying to cover all the bases."

Sam pointed at me. "You're forgetting Willa, the medium. Don't you think you need to include her, just to cover all the bases, as you say?"

"Yeah, I forgot about her. She has to go on the list."

"The problem is not one of them seems to have been in the house when Auggie was killed, except Lucy. There's a piece missing that we have to find, a big piece."

We killed time reading magazines and the newspaper, then Sam restarted a novel he had started a few weeks before, but left in my apartment. At lunchtime I mixed some tuna fish for sandwiches. When one o'clock rolled around, we left for the Historical Society.

We arrived to find another couple was already there, talking to Monty. He saw us enter, and I could see him trying to break away from the others, to no avail, in order to greet us. There was a table set up near the entrance to Monty's office with coffee and soft drinks, so I decided to indulge myself with a beverage. Maybe it would erase any trace of tuna breath.

While I was doing that, Sam examined some of the items on display with price tags on them. He picked up one of them, but I couldn't tell what it was until I got next to him.

"I guess you like that thing. I remember you were looking at it when we were here before. What's the attraction?"

"This is just like one at the Ocean Born Mary house. See, it has the initials *DM* and a number engraved near the handle. This one is *DM8*. The other was *DM3*, I believe."

Monty and the other couple approached us as we were handling the knife. He made no introductions, but slid his hand around the knife handle, easing it out of Sam's hand and placing it back on display.

"I'm so glad you and Sam could make it, Martha."

Somebody once said, *You have to be sincere in business, and if you can fake that, you've got it made.* Monty lived by the idea.

"I thought you were coming later?"

"We were going to, but Sam said he lost interest in the football game, so, what the heck, here we are."

The other man stepped between Monty and Sam, eyeballing the knife. "That's an interesting piece of kitchenware."

Monty switched his gaze to the man. "It certainly is, Mr. Thomas. It's a rare piece, too."

Mr. Thomas lifted the knife gently with both hands, giving careful examination. He tilted it back and forth. "I hate to rain on your parade, Mr. Phillips, but I've seen things like this one before. I'm pretty sure these are made in Asia and can be bought in gift shops most anywhere."

Monty made an indignant noise, stepping closer to the blade. "Oh, no sir, you are mistaken. This was made locally in 1795. Here, notice the marking, *DM8*. That means it was made by David MacAvoy, a Hillsboro metal smith, and it was the eighth such knife he forged. He moved to Henniker, and his descendants donated several of his works to the Historical Society. There can only be a dozen or so like this, and each one was hand crafted. Thus the number eight."

Monty was so quick with his reply that I was inclined to believe him. "Are there others around like this?"

"No, there aren't. The family looked for others, even placing newspaper ads over the years, but they got no responses. I'm sure this is the only one like it left in New England." Monty puffed his chest out, quite pleased with his authoritative explanation.

Monty is quite good at what he does for a living.

Mr. Thomas shook his head. "I don't know, Mr. Phillips. You're the expert around here, but I'll have to keep my eyes open. I still think I've seen stuff like that before."

Monty smiled at him. "Perhaps you've seen some imitations, but I assure you this is an original."

"Okay, if you say so. We're just going to browse around some more," said Mr. Thomas.

"Feel free," said Monty as the couple moved away.

We were silent as Monty clasped his hands behind his back and rocked slightly on his heels. He looked as if he were about to speak, when a group of three women entered the building. "Excuse me, Martha, Sam." Looking content, Monty moved to greet the new arrivals.

I nudged up to Sam and whispered. "So, if this is an original, and there aren't any others around, how do you explain the one at the house?"

"I don't," said Sam. "That is a puzzle, isn't it?" He lifted the knife again and ran his finger over the engraving. Something popped off the knife onto the table. Good thing Monty had moved away.

"Nice work, Slick. Wonder if Monty lives by the phrase, *you break it, you buy it?*" Sam quickly placed it back where he'd found it and edged away from the table. I chuckled and took a closer look at the damage. The piece seemed to crack off the number 8 and was lying on the table beside the knife. *That's funny. The DM8 wasn't engraved at all. It was raised up from the knife's surface, and a fragment cracked off. Sloppy work.*

Sam continued his examination. "That's solder," he said. "And it looks new."

"Why would somebody do that?" I asked.

Sam scratched his chin. "Well, I'm not sure, but it might be a way of changing a marking on a piece of iron."

"Yeah, but I ask again, why? Why change a marking?"

Sam stood silent. His expression told me the wheels in his head were turning.

"Let's bid goodbye to Mr. Phillips and swing by the house. I'm curious about something," he said.

"Got ya. I believe we're thinking the same thing."

We got to the house, entered through the unlocked front door and found Teresa working in the kitchen. Dishes, cups, cutlery, glasses, pots and pans were stacked up at the sink, where she was scrubbing them. She was wearing jeans rolled up at the cuff, an old shirt and blue tennis shoes. Her hair was tied up in a ponytail. *She must have left her legend look in the closet.*

"Hello, Teresa." I gazed at the many items being cleaned. "Why not get Lucy to help you with the cleaning? It's a lot of work for one person." If she was the author of a grand scheme to get her clutches on the house and business, she was also willing to work for it. She was still a puzzle to me, even if her actions when visiting Bart had looked sincere.

"Lucy went upstairs when I showed up, just like yesterday. It's okay with me. What are you two doing today?"

"We just thought we'd take a ride over. I've gotten to really like the old place, and besides, Sam and I were talking about some of the beautiful old pieces here, not the things in the gift shop."

"Well, I've been cleaning some of those things. The stuff's got to be spotless when we open up again."

"When do you expect to do that?" I asked.

"I'm shooting—excuse me, hoping—for two weeks. That should give me enough time to set up some help and give public notice."

"Maybe we can help," said Sam, to my surprise. "Maybe Bart can give you names and phone numbers of his part-time workers. We could help you with calling them." He glanced at me as if seeking my approval. I forced a smile at Teresa.

"Of course," I chimed in. "We'd be glad to help." *Sure, I'd love to call some of Bart's little chippies.*

Sam scooted over to the table where the cutlery was spread out, eyeing the goods. "You know, Teresa, sometime ago I noticed an old kitchen knife with a wooden handle and an engraving, *DM3*. It was about a seven-inch blade, a real beauty. Have you seen it?"

Teresa made a face, examining her memory. "No, I haven't. Everything is right out here on the table. I emptied the drawers in the hutch to clean everything, but you're welcome to double check."

I waltzed over to the hutch and did a fast check, while Sam continued to scan the objects in plain sight.

"Is it something important?" asked Teresa. I sensed a hint of suspicion in her voice.

I answered while crossing the room, before Sam could speak. "No, not really. Sam took a shine to it before and wanted to see it again."

He added to our cover. "I liked it a lot, but didn't have time to ask about it before. It doesn't appear to be here, but I guess it'll show up eventually. No big deal."

"It must have made an impression on you, Sam. If I find it, I'll set it aside and let you know. I'll be sure not to put it in the gift shop and sell it away." She squeaked a giggle.

"Okay," said Sam, "but don't go out of your way. I'll live without it."

To our surprise, a figure appeared in the doorway to the dining room. It was Lucy, looking like a woman who had aged ten years since I'd last saw her. She wore a ragged old house dress and a black scarf over her head. *If I looked that grim, someone would bury me.*

"I heard voices and thought it was you two." Her voice was soft and weak, probably from screaming herself silly when she'd found her dead son, and Bart standing over him with a gun.

I tried to offer condolences. "This thing is just horrible. I'm so sorry about Auggie."

She glared at me as if to say *I'll bet you are.* I would have preferred to slap the old bat but kept my cool.

"I'd like to talk to you, Sam," she said. "This is very important." Her voice took on a civilized tone, one not typical of Lucy. "Upstairs, please. It's private." She sounded downright nice.

Lucy worked her tired body up the stairs, with Sam close behind. I stayed in the kitchen with Teresa.

"I might as well make myself useful. How about I dry off some dishes and pans and put them away?" Teresa gave a nod, and I went to work. She resumed scrubbing what was in the sink.

As I handled the kitchenware, I noticed how beautiful they were. *Old Allan Royston must have acquired them a long time ago. Some of them might have come with the house when he bought it. Could any of them date back to when the Wallaces built the house? If so, they could be worth a good deal of money to antique collectors and dealers. Maybe I should get an appraiser in here and check out the old furnishings. There might be a treasure in the house after all. I'll bet Teresa thought of that, too.*

"Teresa, did Bart or Auggie ever mention anything to you about these old pots and pans and cutlery? I wonder if any came with the house?"

She stopped scrubbing and turned my way. "No, but Lucy did, once. She was in the kitchen, about to cook something in that cast iron skillet, and she held it in both hands. She said that it was older than she was. I asked what she meant, and she said that there were markings on the bottom of some of the cast iron and steel items. The initials *DM* were there. I didn't pay any attention and let it go. I figured, well, old is old."

That's a pretty cavalier attitude from somebody related to a legend.

It seemed to take forever, but Sam eventually re-emerged in the kitchen. He had a gleam in his eye, but not the kind I usually liked to see. "We'd better let you get on with your work, Teresa." He motioned with his index finger for me to make my exit.

"Okay," she answered. "Thanks for coming by and helping."

"We'll be in touch," he said.

Chapter Twenty-Nine
Sunday, September 28, 1975, Henniker, New Hampshire

Sam whisked me out the front door and into the car without answering any of my questions. All he gave me was a tight grin. We were almost into the center of town when he pulled over to the side of the road and turned toward me.

"I know who killed Auggie. I'm sure of it." He was as giddy as a school kid who had just gotten a gold star.

"Okay, are you going to keep me in suspense? Fill me in. If you can clear Bart, I want to know about it." I had asked for Sam's help, so I guessed I had to accept it on his terms. *What is the saying? Be careful what you wish for?*

"You will, dear Martha, you will, but all in good time. Right now, we have to let some time pass and then get back to the Historical Society."

"Let time pass? What the hell for? You're losing me, Sam. Can't you give me a clue?"

"Okay, here's what I can tell you. Lucy needs time to contact Chief Powers and have him meet up with us. Next, she's going to get Teresa to drive the two of them to our meeting as well."

That wasn't much to go on. "Okay, we're going to have a nice get together at the Historical Society for coffee and cookies. Boy, Lucy must have said something awfully interesting to you back at the house. Keep going, please."

"This won't surprise you, but she doesn't think much of Teresa. Lucy thinks she's a whore and a conniver and generally can't be trusted. She said she and Auggie have seen her type before and have even done business with some. Since they were experienced with her type, they felt they knew how to watch out for her if they let her into the business," he said.

"But Auggie was coming around to Teresa. At least he seemed to feel she could be good for the business, and that meant more money. He really liked her performance at the séance."

"Yes," said Sam. "That's what he thought it was, a performance, and so did Lucy. The old gal said it reminded her of some of her own work in various schemes when she was younger. Well, she brought me upstairs to show me something that she had uncovered in Auggie's room. It broke her heart, but didn't surprise her."

Sam paused to catch a breath. "What was it? Don't stop now."

"It's time to move on."

He was about to put the car in gear. "Sam, wait. Are you trying to drive me nuts?"

The car clunked into gear, and we took off. "We'll be there in two minutes, Martha. Hold on."

"This better be good, pal, or you're going to be shut off for a month."

There were a few cars outside the Historical Society, but the only one I recognized was the one with *POLICE* written across the sides. The chief sat behind the wheel with his motor shut off. He opened his door and rose up when he spotted us.

"I hope this is going to please me, Sam. I prefer my Sundays to be slow and easy."

We hadn't taken a step when another car pulled into the lot. It was Teresa and Lucy, an odd couple if I ever saw one.

Cal shook his head. "The gang's all here, right?"

"Right," said Sam. "Let's get the fun going."

We marched inside like a gaggle of geese, me first with Sam right behind. Monty beamed a smile at us as we entered, but his jaw dropped when he saw the rest. Cal held the door for everybody, like he was herding us in.

There were only four others browsing the goods, and the chief turned on his Joe Friday voice to usher them out.

"Excuse me folks, official Police business. I have to ask you to leave now. Perhaps you can come back later." Since they were all adults, they obeyed quietly. If they had been students, I'm sure there would have been protests, although it would have been tame. *This isn't Berkeley.*

There was a tapping sound, probably coming from the old heating pipes, but it could have been Monty's knees knocking. His special Sunday event was turning into something very special, but not the kind of special he wanted.

I threw a glance at Teresa, and she wasn't looking too pleased either. She clearly didn't go for the idea of being near Lucy. Funny, Lucy was the one keeping her distance from Teresa at the house. Now the shoe was on the other foot.

Monty struggled for a proper greeting. "Well, ah, I'm glad to see you all. Thanks for coming. There's plenty of coffee. Help yourself, won't you?"

I waved a negative. Sam did the same, but Cal stepped up to the refreshment table and grabbed a cup. No doughnut, though. He kept in good shape, spoiling the Hollywood cop stereotype.

Sam made his way to the display table where Monty was standing. "Ah, glad to see you haven't sold that knife I like. It sure is a beautiful antique, or at least, it was." He fingered the ends and lifted it up to eye level.

"What do you mean?" asked Monty. "It's an original, hand crafted. I told you that."

Sam turned to face Cal, a few feet away. "Interesting thing, Chief, earlier today a guy was here who insisted that this was a fake. He said he's seen imitations like this elsewhere. But Monty gave a good accounting of the knife's origin and sure convinced me." He swiveled around to Monty. "The only trouble I have is that Monty said it's the only one of a kind, made by the metal smith David MacCoy in 1795."

"That's absolutely true," insisted Monty. "I've done my research, and you can count on it being genuine."

Monty sure hates having his word questioned, especially about his knowledge of historical items.

"Oh, I don't doubt you on that," said Sam. "But here's where I'm having a problem. If it's one of a kind, and I believe it is, then how come I saw one at the Ocean Born Mary house a short while ago, with *DM3* engraved right on it?"

"Ah, there you are, Sam. If there is a DM3 at the house, and thank you for letting me know about it, you're talking about an earlier piece. The one you're holding is DM8." Monty smiled, checking out all the faces, content that he had won the point.

Sam lowered the knife, changing his grip, his right hand clutching the handle. He edged closer to Cal. "You know, Chief, I was a bad boy today. I forgot to mention something to Monty. When I was here earlier, I was checking out this knife—which looks just like the one at the OBM—but it has *DM8* on it. I was running my finger along the initials and oops, I did it again." Sam managed to chip away another piece of solder, just below the other one. "If I didn't know any better, I'd swear this one is really *DM3,* and somebody used solder to try to make the *3* look like an *8.* He went over the *DM* initials, too. What do you think, Chief?"

Cal Powers took the knife from Sam and repeated the examination. More flecks of solder came off the blade, until it was clear that the true initials were *DM3*. The chief was only slightly impressed. "Sam, this proves that Monty is a deceiver, but I don't think I need to clamp the cuffs on him yet. Do you have something more interesting? I sure hope so."

"I believe I do, Chief. Stay with me." He left the knife with Cal and paced over to Lucy. "How many shots did you hear the night Auggie was killed?"

"Two, I heard two I think."

"Yes, Lucy, you heard two. Isn't that right, Chief?"

"Yes, that's correct. There were two bullet wounds in Auggie. So?"

"So what if he didn't die from gunshots?"

A substantial gasp came from the group, but Monty's face grew pale.

"What are you suggesting, Detective Sam?" asked Cal, whose eyebrows reached for the ceiling.

"What if Auggie was stabbed with a knife, a large one with a seven-inch blade, like the one you're holding? What if the killer used a gun to shoot Auggie twice at close range? Wouldn't the gunshot holes mask the knife wound? Couldn't that even fool the medical examiner?"

The chief nodded slowly, tapping a finger on the blade. "Hmm . . . That's possible. There's a way to check. There's a new game in town for law enforcement. It's called, *blood testing;* more specifically, *DNA* testing. We can find even a microscopic amount of blood residue on the knife, if there is any, and the DNA thing can tell us whose blood it is. Are you accusing someone, Sam?" Cal spun his head toward Monty.

"Now wait a minute, you can't be serious. That woman could have done it." Monty glared at Teresa. "She wanted to take over the business and grab the house with it. She must have done it." He backed up against the wall next to his office.

"Greed has often been a motive for murder, Sam," said Cal. "She's big enough to wield a knife and to use a gun."

"Yes, she is, but there's another motive, the strongest of them all—love." There weren't any gasps this time, just some open jaws. "Lucy, if you please."

The old woman reached into the purse strapped over her shoulder. She fumbled with the cover, and her eyes were tearing over as she extracted a folded piece of paper. "Here, Sam, you tell them."

"No, no, please! Don't read that letter!" shouted Monty, his demeanor destroyed in an instant, his hands trembling.

"I don't have to read it," said Sam, as he handed it to the chief. "I'll just sum it up. Monty and Auggie were lovers." Another gasp, this time from Teresa and me.

"Monty was growing jealous of Bart. He feared his close friendship with Auggie was something else, and he was sure of it when he snuck back into the house after the séance, where he found Bart and Auggie hugging. They had been fighting, but made up with drinks and a hug, not unlike other times, according to Bart. But it was too much for Monty. You hid until Bart left to find Teresa, and then you confronted Auggie. He was pretty loaded and still a bit combative. Then you fought. Isn't that how it went?"

Monty was in tears, holding his fists close to his face, as if he could hide that way. "Auggie was toying with me, making fun of me, saying maybe he should try an affair with Bart, that he'd be a better lover than me. What a bastard! Why did he want to hurt me like that? I couldn't take it. I saw the knife nearby and grabbed it. I plunged it into Auggie. Boy, did that smug look of his disappear." He looked like he was going to lose his breakfast.

"You knew Auggie carried a gun," said Sam. "You refer to it in the letter, when you threatened to use it someday. You were still able to conjure up a way of hiding the stab wound. It might have worked, too, if I hadn't taken a shine to that knife before you got the idea to hide in this collection. If you had sold it to a tourist, who knows where it would have gone?"

"You know, Sam, I might have to put you on the payroll one of these days," said the chief as he released a set of handcuffs from his belt. In seconds, he had them on Monty, hands behind his back. "There have been too many murders lately in this little town. I hope this is the end of it, forever. Come along, Phillips, you've got a date with the State Police." Cal recited the rights of the accused man.

"What about Bart?" I pleaded. "Can they let him go now?"

"I'll have to make a couple of calls, and there'll be some red tape to deal with, but maybe we can get him out by tonight. Go home and wait. I'll get back to you."

I pushed past Monty and hugged Chief Powers with all I had. Teresa thanked Cal, too, but not physically. Lucy was lost in a silent cry, her eyes flowing with tears.

"Sam, why don't you drive Teresa back to the house? I'll take Lucy in her car."

Sam gave me a thumbs up.

It was over. Bart was back home, a free man. He and Teresa were making final plans for reopening the house, and Lucy had moved away, unable to live in the house where her son had died. The legend had added a new chapter. The Ocean Born Mary house had been the scene of a recent murder. They were gambling that the public would eat it up.

The Saturday after Bart's release, I took Sam over to the house to see if I could help my brother. It had gotten very cold overnight, probably twenty degrees cooler than the day before. When we parked out front, Sam glanced at the left-front tire.

"Hmmm . . . that puppy looks low to me. Why don't you go on ahead in the house, Martha? I want to check this tire with a gauge. I'll just be a minute."

The front door was unlocked, as usual, so I let myself in. Stepping through the door, I felt a blast of cold air. *Wasn't that supposed to work the other way around?*

I spotted Teresa from behind as she ascended the front stairs. Whatever else I thought of that woman, I admired how she carried herself, almost floating up the stairs.

"Hello, Teresa," I called. No response. *She might be graceful and lithe, but she must also be going deaf. The hell with her.*

Bart's voice was coming from the kitchen, along with female voices, one which I'm sure I recognized as a helper from weeks before. I joined the crowd.

"Hi, Bart, how's it going?" He was about to greet me but stopped, giving me a strange look. "Mart, are you okay? You look weird."

I felt weird. Standing beside him, facing two girls, was Teresa. "Boy, you sure move fast, Teresa."

"What are you talking about?" she answered.

I knew there was a back stairway. *Could she have gone up the front and raced down the back?* "How long have you been in the kitchen?"

She and Bart looked at each other before returning their gaze to me. "About ten minutes. Why?"

My mouth was as dry as it had ever been, and my head began to spin. "Could I trouble you for a glass of water?" I asked one of the girls. She fetched it for me, and I swallowed the liquid quickly. "Oh, nothing," I said, looking at Teresa.

My stare was making her uneasy, I could tell, and my question must have seemed quite strange. "You know, I think this Halloween is going to be one hell of a good time."

About the Author

Although he describes himself as a "card carrying New Englander," Steve lived for twenty-six years in Maryland while pursuing a career spanning four federal agencies. His background has enabled him to serve as a project manager at the National Security Agency, the Environmental Protection Agency, the National Fire Academy and the Centers for Medicare and Medicaid Services, where he worked with teams of experts in various fields to develop state-of-the-art training for both classrooms and distance learning technologies.

A "Baby Boomer," Steve took up fiction writing as he moved into his career final frontier. Married since 1975, a father of three and a grandfather, Steve and his wife Louise own a home on Cape Cod that will serve as his private writer's colony for the years ahead.

His first novel, Connections, was published in 2012 by Gypsy Shadow Publishing, an eBook publisher from Texas. It is the first in a series featuring Detective Jack Contino, battling crime in New England in the 1970's. The other two in the series are Aberration and Calculation. In his fourth mystery, Steve departs from the Det. Jack Contino crime stories and features Sam Miller teaming up in a strange way with Martha Sanborn to solve a murder while hunting for an ex-Nazi in rural New Hampshire.

Steve holds a Master's degree in Educational Technology from Boston University and a B.A. in Business Administration from New England College and spent over thirty years in the Education/Training field, including posts in higher education and the federal government. In 1999 he won a finalist Telly award, for writing, producing and co-hosting a training video on the Emergency Education Network (EENET), a cable network that serves firefighters and law enforcement emergency responders.

Steve has served the Board of Directors for the Cape Cod Writers' Center (CCWC) and holds an administrative position with the Cape Cod Senior Softball League, as well as swinging a quick bat.

WEBSITE: www.stevenmarini.com
TWITTER: https://twitter.com/StevenPMarini
FACEBOOK: https://www.facebook.com/StevenPMarini
BLOG: http://babyboomerspm.blogspot.com

CPSIA information can be obtained
at www.ICGtesting.com
Printed in the USA
FSHW01n1607150618
49176FS

CPSIA information can be obtained
at www.ICGtesting.com
Printed in the USA
FSHW01n1607150618
49176FS